DRAGON SLAYERS' ACADEMY™ 17

HAIL! HAIL! CAMP DRAGONONKA!

By Kate McMullan
Cover illustration by Stephen Gilpin
Illustrated by Bill Basso

Grosset & Dunlap
An Imprint of Penguin Group (USA) Inc.

To *Arlotte-chay Einer-stay*, who has read every
book in the series, including this one
—KM

GROSSET & DUNLAP
Published by the Penguin Group
Penguin Group (USA) Inc., 375 Hudson Street, New York, New York 10014, USA
Penguin Group (Canada), 90 Eglinton Avenue East, Suite 700,
Toronto, Ontario M4P 2Y3, Canada (a division of Pearson Penguin Canada Inc.)
Penguin Books Ltd., 80 Strand, London WC2R 0RL, England
Penguin Group Ireland, 25 St. Stephen's Green, Dublin 2, Ireland
(a division of Penguin Books Ltd.)
Penguin Group (Australia), 250 Camberwell Road, Camberwell, Victoria 3124, Australia
(a division of Pearson Australia Group Pty. Ltd.)
Penguin Books India Pvt. Ltd., 11 Community Centre,
Panchsheel Park, New Delhi—110 017, India
Penguin Group (NZ), 67 Apollo Drive, Rosedale, Auckland 0632, New Zealand
(a division of Pearson New Zealand Ltd.)
Penguin Books (South Africa) (Pty.) Ltd., 24 Sturdee Avenue,
Rosebank, Johannesburg 2196, South Africa

Penguin Books Ltd., Registered Offices: 80 Strand, London WC2R 0RL, England

Cover illustration by Stephen Gilpin.

Text copyright © 2006 by Kate McMullan. Cover illustration copyright © 2012 by
Penguin Group (USA) Inc. Illustrations copyright © 2006 by Bill Basso. This edition
published in 2012 by Grosset & Dunlap, a division of Penguin Young Readers Group,
345 Hudson Street, New York, New York 10014. GROSSET & DUNLAP and DRAGON
SLAYERS' ACADEMY are trademarks of Penguin Group (USA) Inc. Printed in the U.S.A.

Library of Congress Control Number: 2006000558

ISBN 978-0-448-44124-5   10 9 8 7 6 5 4 3 2 1

ALWAYS LEARNING   PEARSON

Chapter I

Dear DSA Lads and Lasses,

Greetings from your headmaster!

Zounds! Was I ever surprised when the School Inspectors showed up and said I had to let you out for summer vacation! In my day, we had no vacations. And look how splendidly I turned out.

I hope you are all happy back at home. Just remember—whatever you do—don't READ!

It weakens the eyes, lads and lasses. And who knows what strange new ideas might creep into your little heads? If you happen to see a book lying about this summer, take my advice and leave it be!

When you come back to DSA next fall, be sure to bring eight pennies for tuition. That's right. Eight! 8! Ocho! Seven won't get so much as your big toe in the door. Nope. It's eight, or you're out. Start saving up!

Me? I'm heading north to revisit the mud wallows of my youth, where I made my mark as a mud wrestling champ.

Ta ta from your favorite headmaster,

Mordred de Marvelous

Dear Headmaster Mordred,

Thank you for writing to me. The Postal Peasant told me that I am the first person in Pinwick ever to get a letter. When I go to the village now, folks point and say, "That's the lad what got a letter."

I told my father about the eight pennies for DSA tuition. After he stopped laughing, he said the only way he can pay is in cabbages. How many might it take, sir?

With hope,

Wiglaf of Pinwick

Dear Wiglaf,

Are you having fun this summer? I'm not. I can't wait to get back to DSA!

Being a full-time princess is the worst. This morning, Mumsy had me take a milk bath to make my skin soft. Now I smell like a cow. Next, I took a harp lesson and broke six strings. Then it was off to a fair, where I judged a Turnip Soup Contest—and dribbled soup down the front of my gown. It is the fourth gown I have ruined this week!

There was a jousting tournament, too— but I had to sit in the stands and watch. It was torture. How I long to put on my Sir Lancelot armor and take up my sword again!

My only friends here at the palace are Lancelot, Arthur, and Guinevere—my goldfish. They listen to my woes. But they cannot talk to me. I miss you, Wiggie. Write me back and tell me what you are up to.

Yours till butter flies,

Erica

Dear Erica,

My father was most surprised when I came home last week. He'd never heard of summer vacation. When I told him what it was, he said it sounded like a fine idea and he took to his hammock.

That leaves me to fetch water, weed the cabbage patch, chop wood, and rake pig dung.

Our hovel is crowded and loud. My father never stops belching. My mother never stops fretting. And my twelve brothers never stop fighting and yelling and punching. That is why I sleep in the pigsty with Daisy.

Write to me again soon!

Your friend,

Wiglaf

Dear Wiglaf,

Greetings from thine DSA librarian. How I hopeth thine summer is filled with laughter and good books.

Summer vacation gaveth me the chance to cometh to the Frankfurter Book Fair. I haveth bought many a fine book, such as:

The Short Walk by Earl B. Homesoon

Knocking at Your Door by Gus Who

The fair endeth tomorrow. Then I shalt stay with my Little Brothers of the Peanut Brittle until school resumeth in the fall. I looketh forward to seeing thee then, Wiglaf.

I remain,

Brother Dave

Dear Brother Dave,

Thank you for writing to me. How I would love to go to a book fair!

Daisy and I are enjoying the library books we checked out for the summer. I am halfway through The Very Scary Thursday by Gladys Friday, and Daisy has just started The Day Rover Ran Away by Hewlett D. Dawgout.

Your student,

Wiglaf

Dear Wiglaf,

I hope your summer is better than mine. My mother means well, but she is driving me crazy. She says both of us must slim down, so she has put us on an awful diet. We eat carrot tops and celery leaves. And we drink barley tea. What I wouldn't give for a big platter of Frypot's scrambled eel right now!

Has your father told you any new knock-knocks? I hope so. I can't wait to hear them!

Tell Daisy ello-hay for me.

Yours till rivers run,

Angus

Dear Angus,

Daisy says to tell you ello-hay, too.

I worry about my dear pig. No one in my family knows she can talk. I remind her not to speak in front of anyone—especially my mother. You know how superstitious she is. If Molwena were to hear a pig speak, she would think the world was coming to an end!

How I wish you could come visit me! My mother's cabbage soup would slim you down in no time—if you could choke it down.

My father sends you this joke:

Knock knock!
Who's there?
Luke.

Luke who?
Luke out for falling rocks!

Your friend,

Wiglaf

Hiya, Wiggie!

Guess what? I got home and found that my house was gone! Mom had it torn down. She is having a new, bigger, grander house built. It will have something called a "toilet." I am not sure what that is, but Mom is excited to have the first one in Gildengeld. It is a mess here. There are carpenters and stone masons all over the place.

None of my friends are around. All I do is look after my baby brother Bibs because the nursemaids all quit after an hour with him. Bibs is a horror!

Tell your dad I've been practicing

my belching. Zounds, I am loud!
Next time I see him, I shall challenge
him to a contest. Boy, do I miss you,
Wiggie!

Your good buddy,

Janice

Dear Janice,

How I wish I might see your new house. I am not sure, but I think a toilet is a basin used to clean mud off boots.

This morning, my mother looked up at the sky and saw a dark cloud shaped like a potato. She ran into our hovel, shouting that it was a bad omen. She has not come out again.

When I told my father that you wish to challenge him to a belching contest, he belched so loudly that you must have heard it up in Gildengeld! My left ear is still ringing.

I miss you, too.

Your friend,

Wiglaf

Chapter 2

Wiglaf sat down on a bale of hay beside Daisy. He opened Angus's latest letter. The news from Piffledown was not good. Angus's mom had cooked dandelion stew for supper.

Just then, Wiglaf's father stuck his head into the sty.

"Knock knock!" cried Fergus.

Wiglaf looked up. "Who's there?" he answered.

"Juicy!" roared Fergus.

"Juicy who?" asked Wiglaf.

"Juicy the size of that rat?" cried Fergus.

"Rat?" Wiglaf jumped up. "What rat?"

Daisy squealed, *"At-ray?"* And she jumped

up, too.

"Gotcha!" cried Fergus. And when he finally stopped laughing, he added, "Soup's on." Then he turned and left the sty.

Wiglaf patted his pig. "Daisy, you must remember not to speak in front of anyone."

"*Orry-say*," said Daisy. "*I-yay as-way ared-scay.*"

"I know, but if my mother were to hear you..." Wiglaf did not need to say more.

Daisy nodded and nuzzled Wiglaf's face. Then she trotted off to the riverbank where the wildflowers grew.

Wiglaf hurried down the hill to the hovel. He opened the door—and nearly shut it again.

His twelve beefy, yellow-haired brothers were having another head-banging contest.

His eldest brother lurched forward and clonked his noggin on the table. BONK!

The second-eldest did the same. BONK!

Wiglaf, the third-eldest, only stared.

The fourth-eldest slammed his head on the table. BONK!

The fifth-eldest went next: BONK!

"BAM-O!" cried the sixth-eldest as he smashed his skull onto the table. BONK! "I did it the hardest!" he shouted. "I win!"

"Enough!" yelled Molwena. "You'll dent my table." She threw a pinch of salt over her shoulder for good luck.

Wiglaf tried to sit down at the end of a bench.

"Beat it!" said the eldest, jabbing him with an elbow.

"Don't come over here, Wiggie!" shouted the youngest brother from across the table. "You smell funny!"

"It's 'cause he took a bath," yelled the second-youngest, holding his nose.

"Eat!" commanded Molwena.

But no one paid her any mind.

"Sit by me, Wiggie," called Dudwin. He scooted over and made room on the bench. "I think you smell fine."

Wiglaf sat down next to Dudwin. He peered into the soup pot. It was empty.

"Here." Dudwin slid over his own bowl, which had a little soup left inside. "You can have the rest." He gave Wiglaf his spoon.

"Thanks, Dudwin," said Wiglaf. He took a sip. Gaaack! The soup's foul taste always came as an awful surprise.

"Tell us about how you slew the dragon Gorzil, Wiggie," said Dudwin.

"He told us that," said the eldest.

"He didn't finish," said Dudwin. "Tell us, Wiggie."

"All right," said Wiglaf. "Gorzil was a wicked dragon. He belched out clouds of black smoke."

"BURRP!" belched Fergus from his place at the head of the long table. But no smoke appeared.

"BURRRP!" belched the eldest.

"BURRRRP!" belched the second-eldest.

"Gorzil shot red-hot flames from his snout," Wiglaf shouted over the belching.

"Red-hot dragon snot!" cried the fourth-youngest brother.

All his brothers picked up the chant: "Red-hot dragon snot!"

"Did you get splatted with dragon snot, Wiggie?" shouted the eldest.

"No," said Wiglaf. But no one heard him. They were all laughing too hard.

Suddenly, the hovel door banged open. The laughing stopped.

Daisy ran into the room, followed by a swarm of buzzing bees.

"Elp-hay! Elp-hay!" Daisy cried.

Molwena screamed.

All twelve brothers jumped to their feet, overturning the table.

"Ave-say e-may!" Daisy cried as she galloped around the overturned table, the bees close behind. *"Elp-hay e-may, Iggie-way!"*

"Blazing King Ken's britches!" cried Fergus. His eyes were as wide as saucers. "The pig speaks Pig Latin!"

"The pig is possessed!" cried Molwena. "We are doomed!" She began grabbing fistfuls of salt and heaving them over her shoulder.

The brothers ran around swatting madly at bees, and at each other. "Kill the bees! Kill the bees!" they yelled.

Wiglaf grabbed Daisy and pulled her into a corner of the hovel, out of harm's way. Molwena went after the bees with her broom, chasing them outside.

"*I-yay ot-gay ung-stay!*" cried Daisy over all the noise. Fat tears rolled down her cheeks.

"You got stung?" said Wiglaf. "Where?"

Daisy turned her haunch toward him, and Wiglaf yanked the stinger out.

Daisy wiped a tear from her cheek with the back of a hoof. "*Ank-thay ou-yay, Iggie-way.*"

"WIGLAF!" boomed Fergus. "WHY DOES YOUR PIG SPEAK IN THIS STRANGE TONGUE?"

All twelve brothers and his mother waited for his answer.

"Um, you see, I met this wizard Zelnoc, and—and he sort of put a speech spell on Daisy," Wiglaf stammered. "But the wizard's spell went wrong. So Daisy speaks Pig Latin."

"A wizard?" cried Molwena. "Doom is near!" She had used up all the salt, so she picked up a spoon and tossed it over her shoulder.

CLONK! The spoon hit the second-eldest on the head. He grabbed it up and threw it at the third-eldest. CLONK! The third-eldest threw it at the fourth-eldest. CLONK! Spoons were flying now: CLONK! CLONK! CLONK! Other brothers piled on and soon a brawl was underway.

Only Dudwin stood apart from the others, looking at Daisy with awe.

"The pig must go, Fergie!" cried Molwena. "She'll bring bad luck down on our heads! And we have enough bad luck already!"

"You heard your mother, Wiglaf," Fergus said. "The pig must go."

"Father, no!" cried Wiglaf.

Daisy hung her head and walked slowly toward the hovel door.

"You know your mother, Son," Fergus said, keeping his voice low. "She won't rest until she's seen the last of that pig."

Wiglaf folded his arms across his chest. "If Daisy goes, I go, too," he said.

"No!" cried Dudwin.

Fergus belched sadly and said, "Sorry, lads. What your mother says goes." Wiglaf and Daisy left the hovel. They climbed up the hill to the sty.

"*I-yay am-yay orry-say,*" Daisy said.

Wiglaf patted his pig. "You could not help it," he said.

"*Ere-way all-shay e-way o-gay?*" she asked.

"I know not where we shall go, Daisy," said Wiglaf. "Only away from here."

In the sty, Wiglaf spread out his thin brown blanket and tossed his few belongings on it: his lucky rag, his sword, his water flask. Then he bundled up his blanket.

"Ready, Daisy?" said Wiglaf.

"*Eady-ray,*" said Daisy.

They set off from the sty. As they passed the hovel, Dudwin ran outside.

"Wiggie!" he cried. "Take me with you!"

Molwena raced outside and grabbed him. "You're staying right here, Duddy," she said.

"Rats!" said Dudwin.

Wiglaf smiled. "I shall miss you, Dud."

"Don't let any black cats cross your path, Wiggie," said Molwena. "Don't walk under any ladders." She gave him a hug that nearly squeezed the breath out of him. "Come home again soon—but don't bring any talking beasts!"

Fergus stepped out of the hovel and called, "Knock knock!"

Wiglaf groaned and said, "Who's there?"

"Justin!" bellowed Fergus.

"Justin who?" said Wiglaf.

"Justin case you get hungry," Fergus said, and he thrust a flask of cabbage soup into

Wiglaf's hand.

Then Wiglaf and his pig set off down the path. Where would they go?

Wiglaf had no idea. When school first let out, he had felt so free and happy. Now he wished there was no such thing as summer vacation.

Chapter 3

"Daisy! I have it!" said Wiglaf as he and his pig reached the Swamp River. "We shall go to the Royal Palace and visit Erica."

The short-legged pig looked doubtful. "*At-thay is-yay a-yay ong-lay alk-way,*" she said.

"'Twas a long walk from DSA," said Wiglaf. "But 'tis not so far from here. You know how grateful the queen is to you for saving King Ken. I think she shall be happy to put us up for a day or two."

On the two trudged, Daisy on her short legs, and Wiglaf on his longer ones.

They saw no one else as they headed north on the path beside the river. Yet

Wiglaf sometimes had a strange feeling that someone was following them. Robbers and fierce creatures often lurked beside the river. He picked up the pace.

They had walked for a good distance when the light began to fade from the sky.

SNAP!

Wiglaf spun around. Was that a twig snapping?

There was no one behind them.

Still, Wiglaf was sure he heard footsteps.

"*Iglaf-way?*" whispered Daisy. "*I-yay ave-hay a-yay unny-fay eeling-fay.*"

"I have a funny feeling, too," Wiglaf whispered.

Daisy nodded. She looked scared.

But on they walked, singing songs in Pig Latin to keep up their spirits.

"*Inkle-tway, inkle-tway
Ittle-lay ar-stay,*

Ow-hay I-yay onder-way
At-whay ou-yay are-yay..."

When the sun went down, a half moon lit the sky. Wiglaf saw that Daisy was tired.

"We shall sleep here beside the river, Daisy," Wiglaf told her.

Daisy looked around warily. *"I-yay ill-way eep-slay under-yay at-thay ee-tray,"* she said. She trotted off toward a large oak.

Wiglaf spread his thin brown blanket on the ground. He took off his boots and lay down. Things unseen scurried through the nearby woods. Far away, a wolf howled.

Wiglaf rolled himself up in his blanket. He tried counting sheep. He had reached seventy-six and had nearly drifted off when—SNAP!

What was that?

Someone was creeping through the brush. He was sure of it.

"Daisy?" he called softly.

No answer.

The footsteps grew louder.

Wiglaf's heart was pounding. Was he about to be robbed? He scooted way down inside his blanket. He hoped he looked like a large brown log.

He peeked out from his blanket. He saw a shadow! It was coming closer and closer!

"Who—who goes there?" Wiglaf stammered.

"Me!" a voice shouted out in the night.

"Me who?" asked Wiglaf.

"Me Dudwin," said the voice. "That's who."

"Dudwin?" Wiglaf struggled out of his blanket and sat up. He was not sure whether to be mad or glad that it was his brother and not a robber.

"Surprise, Wiggie!" said Dudwin, grinning. "I followed you."

"So I see," said Wiglaf.

"Wherever you're going, I want to go, too," Dudwin said. "Remember what fun we had when we went to the Cave of Doom?"

"Sort of." What Wiglaf really remembered was rescuing Dudwin from one scrape after another.

"Remember how I saved us from the troll?" said Dudwin. "Remember how I threw cabbage soup in his face?"

"I remember." Wiglaf sighed. Dudwin was a good lad. But he had a way of stirring things up.

"Can I share your blanket, Wiggie?" asked Dudwin.

Wiglaf nodded. Before long, both lads were snoring softly.

The next morning, Daisy trotted back to Wiglaf's campsite.

"*Udwin-day!*" exclaimed the surprised pig.

"Hi, Daisy!" Dudwin said. "I don't think you are possessed. And guess what? Wherever you're going, I'm going, too."

The three finished off the cabbage soup. Then they took up their journey to the palace.

They had walked for a couple of hours when Dudwin stopped. "Look, Wiggie," he said, pointing to a large oak ahead on the path. "A message tree."

"So it is," said Wiglaf.

The three went over for a closer look.

"What do they say?" asked Dudwin.

Wiglaf read the messages tied to the tree branches out loud:

King Ken is a yammering,
ale-headed nit-wit.

King Ken is a goat-bearded
Banbury cheese.

King Ken is a festering blister
on the heel of the kingdom.

"*Oor-pay Ing-kay En-kay,*" said Daisy.

"He is not very popular," said Wiglaf.

"What does this say, Wiggie?" asked
Dudwin. He pulled a piece of parchment
from a thick stack nailed to the tree trunk
and handed it to his brother.

Wiglaf read aloud:

ARE YOU A NATURE-LOVING
LAD OR LASS?
DO YOU LIKE HEALTHY OUTDOOR
EXERCISE?
DO YOU LIKE TO SWIM?
MAKE THINGS IN ARTS AND CRAFTS?
WIN PRIZES?
SING SONGS?
TOAST MARSHMALLOWS OVER A

ROARING CAMPFIRE?
YES?
THEN COME TO
CAMP DRAGONONKA,
FOR A SUMMER YOU'LL NEVER FORGET

Yes! Wiglaf was indeed a nature-loving lad. Yes! He wanted a summer he'd never forget. A summer filled with sun and fun. He could almost taste the toasted marshmallows.

"It sounds great," said Wiglaf.

"Camp!" shouted Dudwin. "I'll love camp!"

"*E-may oo-tay,*" said Daisy.

There was small print under the large print.

ALL THIS FOR ONLY 3 PENNIES

"Three pennies?" Wiglaf cried. Why did everything cost so much? And why did his family have so little? "We cannot go."

"We have to go, Wiggie!" said Dudwin. "I know—we'll sneak in."

Some extra-small print at the bottom of the parchment caught Wiglaf's eye. He read:

Bring three friends and you can come for FREE!

"Hooray!" shouted Dudwin. "All we have to do is find three friends!"

"Three friends would get one of us to camp," said Wiglaf.

"You shall think of something, Wiggie," said Dudwin. "You always do."

Wiglaf began to think. He had three friends. Erica, Angus, and Janice. Three friends who were not enjoying summer vacation. Three friends who could afford to pay three pennies. It was not a plan, exactly. But it was a start. His heart began to beat with excitement. He folded the parchment and tucked it into his tunic pocket. Perhaps there was a chance that he and Daisy and Dudwin and his friends might all go to this wonderful place—Camp Dragononka.

Chapter 4

The sun was high in the sky when Wiglaf, Dudwin, and Daisy reached the palace.

"Yowie!" shouted Dudwin, gawking at the tall pink marble towers. "This is some hovel!"

Wiglaf stepped up to the iron gates and called, "Guards!"

A guard in a red tunic with the royal crest on the front hurried over to open the gate. But when he saw the trio standing before him, he shouted, "Be gone, peasants! You are allowed inside these gates only on King Ken's Crowning Day. Come back in two months, peasants."

"But we have come to see Princess Erica, sir," said Wiglaf.

"She's my friend, too," said Dudwin.

"The princess? I don't think so," the guard said snottily. "Be gone, riff-raff!"

Daisy's eyes widened. "*Iff-raff-ray?*" she cried. And she charged past the guard through the gate, galloping toward the palace.

"Go, Daisy!" shouted Dudwin. He and Wiglaf took off running after the pig, nearly knocking over the guard.

"Stop!" called the guard. "Stop, varlets!" He blew on a golden whistle.

Instantly, the palace yard filled with red-coated guards.

"Arrest them!" shouted the first guard.

A guard grabbed Wiglaf.

Another grabbed Dudwin.

"Let go of me!" shouted Dudwin. "Let go,

I say!" He wriggled and struggled and yelled.

Daisy squealed as a guard threw a rope around her neck.

The queen stuck her head out of a high window. "What in the name of St. Dominic's dog is going on down there?" she cried.

"Trespassers, Your Majesty," called the chief guard. "We are taking them to the dungeon."

Queen Barb squinted down at the prisoners. "Daisy?" she called. "Is that you?"

"*Es-yay, our-Yay ajesty-May!*" called Daisy.

"Guards, release them at once!" cried the Queen.

"Y-yes, Your Majesty," muttered the chief guard. He lifted the rope from around Daisy's neck.

"I shall be right down," called the queen. She disappeared from the window.

Daisy frowned and glowered at the guard.

"*I-yay aved-say ing-Kay en-Kay om-fray e-thay ox-pay!*" she said.

"She saved King Ken from the pox," Wiglaf told the guard.

"Oh, you're *that* pig?" exclaimed the guard. "So sorry!" He bowed to Daisy.

"*At-thay's etter-bay,*" said Daisy.

Now Queen Barb swept out of the palace.

"Good day, Your Majesty," said Wiglaf, bowing. "May I present my brother, Dudwin?"

"Welcome to the Royal Palace, lads," said Queen Barb. She held her queenly hand out to be kissed. "And welcome back, Daisy. Oh, King Ken will be so sorry to have missed you. He's off visiting King Bob of Bobbinshire. He's hoping to get some advice on how to be more popular." The queen shrugged. "Well, you're here to see Princess Erica, I'll wager."

"Yes, Your Majesty," said Wiglaf.

"Let me think. Erica had Curtsying Class at ten. Advanced Napkin Folding at eleven." Queen Barb checked the tiny hourglass she wore on a golden chain around her neck. "Princess Manners at lunchtime...She must be in the music chamber now, hosting a tea party for her cousins, Princess Mitzie, Princess Bitsie, and Princess Ditsy."

"Erica? Hosting a tea party?" said Wiglaf, surprised.

"Yes," said the queen. "Now, Daisy!" she went on, turning to the pig. "Would you like to spend some time at the Royal Spa?"

Daisy's eyes lit up. *"Es-yay! Ease-play!"*

The queen led the way into the palace and up the marble stairway of the South Tower. At the top of the stairs, she said, "The music chamber is down the hall to the right. I'll stop by as soon as I get Daisy settled at the spa."

Wiglaf and Dudwin walked down the marble hallway and stopped outside the chamber. They heard high-pitched voices. And laughter. Wiglaf peeked around the door frame. He spotted Erica right away. But she did not look much like the Erica he knew. Her hair was in ringlets and she wore a silky blue gown. She was pouring tea from a silver teapot.

A princess in a purple gown was holding out her cup.

Wiglaf was not sure about going into a room of tea-drinking princesses.

But Dudwin barged right in. "Hi, Princess Erica," he said. "Remember me?"

Erica's mouth dropped open in surprise.

"Dudwin! Wiggie!" she cried. As she raced to greet them, the teapot fell from her hand. The lid snapped open, and tea sloshed all over the princess in purple.

"My new gown!" cried the princess. "It's ruined!"

"Oops!" said Erica. "Sorry, Mitzie."

A princess in a yellow gown glared at Erica. "I think you did it on purpose because Mitzie's gown is prettier than yours."

"Bitsy!" said Erica. "I did not!"

A princess in a green gown picked up a piece of cake and mashed it into the lacy front of Erica's gown.

"Now your gown is ruined, too," she said. "So there!"

Erica scooped up some icing with her finger and popped it into her mouth. "Mmmm," she said, grinning. "That wasn't a very princessy thing to do, Ditsy."

"This is the worst tea party ever!" cried Mitzie.

"Totally the worst," said Bitsy.

"Worse than the worst," said Ditsy.

Just then Queen Barb stuck her head in at the door. "Good heavens!" she exclaimed.

Mitzie, Bitsy, and Ditsy princess-walked over to the queen.

"It's all Cousin Erica's fault!" said Bitsy.

"She wrecked my gown!" said Mitzie.

"We're not coming back here, Aunt Barb," said Ditsy. "You can't make us!"

The three princesses princess-walked out of the music chamber.

"Dear me!" exclaimed Queen Barb when they had gone. "What was all that about?"

Erica sighed. "I messed up again, Mumsy."

The queen gave her a squeeze. "Worry not, darling," she said. "Your friends shall cheer you up."

"We shall, Your Majesty," said Wiglaf. "What do you think of this, Erica?" He pulled the Camp Dragononka parchment from his pocket and handed it to her.

"I saw this on the Royal Message Tree," said Erica. "Sounds like fun, doesn't it?"

"Let me see," said Queen Barb. She took the parchment from Erica and began reading.

"Are you going to this camp, Wiglaf?" the queen asked.

"I hope so, Your Majesty," Wiglaf said. He explained that it cost three pennies, but if he brought three friends, he could go for free.

"I'll bet Angus would like to go," said Erica. "And Janice. They're not having any fun this summer." She turned to the queen. "Mumsy? May I go to camp with Wiglaf? Please?"

The queen looked around the chamber. The royal teapot lay on the floor, dented. The front of Erica's gown was a mess of icing and crumbs.

"Camp!" exclaimed the queen. "What an

excellent idea. I shall command Fawnsley to pack your things immediately."

"I want to go, too!" Dudwin cried. He fell to his knees before the queen. "Oh, Your Most Beautiful Majesty Highness Queen, can you spare three pennies so that a poor peasant lad can go to camp?"

"Dudwin!" cried Wiglaf. His face turned scarlet.

But Queen Barb only laughed. "I shall command the royal treasurer to give you three pennies, Dudwin."

"Oh, thank you, Your Majesty," said Dudwin. He jumped to his feet. "All right!" he cried. "We're going to camp!"

Chapter 5

he next morning, Wiglaf, Dudwin, Erica, and Daisy set off from the palace. They headed for Angus's hometown of Piffledown.

Wiglaf carried his things at the end of a stick, bundled in his thin brown blanket.

Dudwin carried the thick royal blue blanket the queen had given him over his shoulder. He jingled his three pennies in his pocket.

All Erica carried was a box from the palace pastry chef. The Royal Coachmen were driving her trunks directly to Camp Dragononka.

"*I-yay ove-lay aths-bay,*" said Daisy as she trotted along beside Wiglaf. She was pinker than ever after her time at the spa.

"Oh, I shall never take a bath," said Dudwin. "Pa says baths cause madness."

"*Onsense-nay,*" said Daisy.

"How glad I am that you showed up at the palace, Wiggie," said Erica. Her hair was braided once more. She had on a tunic. Strapped around her middle was her Sir Lancelot tool belt, with all sorts of useful items hanging from it. "I am just not cut out for princess duties."

They walked until midday when Dudwin said, "My feet hurt!"

"Not much further," said Wiglaf. "Look. Piffledown is straight ahead."

A milkmaid came toward them on the path. She was leading a cow.

"Excuse me, milkmaid," said Wiglaf.

"Where do Turnipia du Pangus and her son Angus live?"

"In that large thatched-roof cottage," said the milkmaid, pointing. "But if you wait here, they shall be by in a moment."

No sooner had she spoken than a big woman with a knot of blond hair on top of her head came jogging up the path.

Angus came jogging down the path behind her.

"Pick up the pace, Poopsie Pie," called the woman, huffing and puffing. "Remember—no pain, no gain."

"Gaaaaaa," said Angus, panting for breath.

"Hallo, Angus," said Wiglaf as the two ran closer. "Hello, Lady Turnipia."

Angus stared at Wiglaf and stopped dead in his tracks.

"Jesters' bells!" he exclaimed. "All this

exercise is making me see things!"

"Why, it's your school friends!" exclaimed Turnipia. "Jog in place while you talk to them, dear."

Angus moved his feet slightly.

"Jogging is the latest way to slim down," Turnipia told them. "And eating parsley, carrot tops, and celery soup."

"Yuck," said Dudwin.

"Yuck is right," said Angus. "It's awful!"

"Join us for lunch, please!" said Turnipia.

"Just don't expect anything that will fill your belly," Angus muttered as Turnipia jogged off toward the cottage.

"How happy I am to see all of you!" Angus said. He scratched Daisy behind the ears. Then they began walking toward the cottage. "What brings you here?"

"We wanted to show you this," said Wiglaf. He handed Angus the parchment.

Angus read it eagerly.

"Zounds! Camp Dragononka sounds excellent," he said. "Are you going?"

"I hope to," Wiglaf said.

"I'm going," said Erica. "Why don't you come, too, Angus?"

"Mother would never let me." Angus sighed and handed the parchment back to Wiglaf. "Not in a million years."

"But why?" asked Wiglaf.

"She is so happy I'm home for the summer," he said. "If I told her I wanted to go off to camp, it would break her heart." He sighed again. "But I don't know how much more jogging and dieting I can take!"

"Poor Angus!" said Erica.

Angus nodded. "Write to me," he said. "Tell me everything about camp. Especially what you have to eat."

When they reached the cottage, Angus

opened the gate and let them into the yard.

Turnipia was talking to a neighbor lady over the fence.

"Take your friends inside, Angus," Turnipia called. "I'm just having a word with Radishia."

As Wiglaf headed for the cottage, he could not help but overhear the two ladies.

"I am off to Lady Thinwisp's Slimming Center this very afternoon!" said Radishia.

"How fortunate you are!" cried Turnipia.

"They say that chubby damsels go in, and slim damsels come out." Radishia giggled. "Why don't you come with me?"

"I long to go!" said Turnipia. "But how can I? It would break little Angus's heart if I were to go off and leave him with his cousins."

"Pity," said Radishia. "Well, ta ta!"

"Excuse me, Lady Turnipia," Wiglaf said

as she neared the cottage. "I could not help but hear what you and your neighbor said."

"Don't worry, lad," Turnipia said. "I'm not running off and leaving my little Angus."

"Let me show you something," Wiglaf said. He handed the camp parchment to Turnipia. "Erica and my brother and I are on our way to this camp. Do you think Angus might like to come with us?"

"Healthy outdoor exercise," Turnipia read. "Swimming and hiking." She looked at Wiglaf. "Why, this is just what Angus needs!"

Then her face fell. "Oh, but he would miss me so terribly. I doubt he would agree to go."

"Shall we ask him?" said Wiglaf.

Turnipia smiled. "Let's!"

Wiglaf followed Turnipia into the

cottage kitchen. Erica was ladling out celery soup. Dudwin was carrying bowls to the table. Angus was setting out soup spoons.

Turnipia hurried over to her son. "I want to ask you something, Poopsie Pie," she said.

"Mother!" wailed Angus. "Don't call me that!"

"Touchy, touchy," said Turnipia. "Tell me, Angus. Would you like to go to this Camp Dragononka with your friends?"

"Me?" cried Angus. "Go to camp?"

Turnipia turned to Wiglaf. "See? What did I tell you? He doesn't want to go."

"What?" cried Angus. "No!"

"You don't have to go, dear," said Turnipia.

"I mean yes!" said Angus. "Yes, I want to go. Please! Send me to camp!"

"Really, darling?" said Turnipia. "You're sure?"

"Yes, yes!" Angus grinned. "Camp sounds

absolutely great!"

"Well!" Turnipia said. "I'd better run out and tell Radishia that I'm coming with her after all."

By the time the soup bowls had been washed and dried, Angus was packed for Camp Dragononka. And Turnipia was packed for Lady Thinwisp's Slimming Center.

Chapter 6

"Whoa!" Radishia called to her horse. She pulled her wagon to a stop just outside Gildengeld, where Janice lived.

Angus and his friends jumped out.

"Ta ta!" Turnipia called, waving. "Have fun at camp!"

The minute the wagon was out of sight, Angus said, "Who's got food?"

Erica opened the box from the royal pastry chef.

Daisy sniffed at the delicate pastries. *"Eam-cray uffs-pay!"* she cried.

"Cream puffs!" crooned Angus, stuffing one into his mouth. "Zounds! I'd forgotten what real food tastes like."

The cream puffs vanished in no time. Then Wiglaf and his friends hiked up the hill to Gildengeld.

Just outside the town, two shepherds came by, with a small flock of sheep.

"Excuse me, shepherds," said Wiglaf. "Where does Squire Smotherbottom live?"

"Can't miss it," said the first shepherd. "It's the biggest house in Gildengeld."

"And it isn't even finished yet," added the second shepherd.

"Smotherbottom used to be a peasant like us, you know," said the first shepherd.

"But he got rich," said the second. "Now he thinks he's a bloody squire. He's even having a statue made of himself!"

The shepherds cracked up laughing at this, and went on their way.

"Let's go," said Angus. "It can't be hard

to find."

Wiglaf and the others walked down the main street of Gildengeld. At last they came to a huge, half-built house. In the yard, a sculptor was chipping away at a hunk of stone. A big-boned man sat on a horse in front of him.

"That's Janice's father," whispered Angus.

Dudwin ran ahead and knocked at the door. Janice opened it. She had bandages on her face and neck and arms.

"All right!" she exclaimed when she saw her friends. "I thought it was the new nursemaid."

Janice was chewing a wad of gum and holding the biggest, baldest baby Wiglaf had ever seen.

"Whooooo!" whooped the baby with glee.

"Come in," yelled Janice over the baby's whoops. "Watch your step. It's crazy in here."

Workers were everywhere, measuring and hammering and sawing. "What are you guys doing here?" Janice yelled over the noise.

"We came to see if you want to go to camp with us!" Wiglaf shouted.

Angus handed her the parchment.

"I'll hold the baby while you read it," offered Wiglaf, who liked babies.

"Be careful," Janice said as she handed him the baby. "Bibs bites."

Bibs grinned, showing two upper teeth and two on the bottom.

Janice read the parchment and looked up. "Gee, I'd love to go," she said. "But who would take care of Bibs? We've been through nearly all the nursemaids in the county."

"Whoooo!" whooped Bibs as Janice took him back.

Just then, there was a knock at the door.

Janice opened it. On the stoop stood a tall woman. Next to her sat a large trunk.

"Aunt Gert!" Janice exclaimed.

"Have someone bring in my trunk, Janice," said Aunt Gert, stepping inside. "I've come to stay. Ever since Giles exploded, I've been alone. I need company. And something to do."

"How about baby-sitting?" asked Janice.

"Love to," said Aunt Gert. She threw open her arms. "Bibsy!"

"Whoooo!" whooped Bibs as he threw his chubby arms around his old aunt's leathery neck and took a bite. She didn't seem to notice.

Janice turned to her friends. She snapped her gum loudly and cried, "Camp Dragononka! Here we come!"

Wiglaf and his friends spent the night at Janice's half-built house. In the morning, the cook fixed them a hearty breakfast of fried noodle pudding and sent them on their way.

A map on the back of the parchment showed the way to Camp Dragononka. The party walked north on Unicorn Path. At last they came to Watchyerstep Woods.

"We take this trail through the woods," said Wiglaf, looking at the map. "It will lead us to Dragononka Ridge."

Into the woods they went.

"It is dark here," said Janice.

"Darker than the Dark Forest," said Erica.

Because of the odd name of the woods, Wiglaf watched his step on the trail. So did the others. And that is why they were taken so completely by surprise when a wiry little man jumped out from behind a tree trunk and yelled, "Sur-prise!"

"*Ikes-yay!*" cried Daisy.

The little man had wild white hair and a long, tangled beard.

"Crazy Looey here," the little man said. "Part-time lunatic, full-time hermit. Maybe you've heard of me?"

"We—we met you once, sir," Wiglaf said when he had found his voice. "On our way to the Cave of Doom."

"The Cave of Doom?" cried the hermit. "Why, that's where I lost my mind. You haven't found it, have you?"

Wiglaf and the others shook their heads.

"Too bad," said the hermit. "And now I've lost my map! How can I find the gold without my map? And how can I find anything without my mind? Woe is me!"

"What's he talking about?" Janice said.

"Who knows?" Angus whispered back.

Now the hermit's face brightened. "Well,

at least I don't have to worry about the terrible curse," he said. "That's a good thing. Hee hee!" He began skipping around in a circle, singing,

"Lost my map, lost my mind,
Hope I won't lose my behind!"

Still singing, Crazy Looey skipped off into the trees.

"That is one nutty hermit," said Janice when he was gone.

They set off through the woods again.

"I'm hungry," said Angus. It was way past lunchtime, and they had not had a bite to eat since breakfast at Janice's house.

But they had no food, so they walked on. They had not gone far when they heard voices ahead of them on the trail.

"Alas and alack!" someone wailed. "'Tis all over my new boot!"

"Here. Scrape it off with these leaves,"

said another voice. "And hurry up about it! We don't want to be left behind."

Wiglaf and his friends rounded a bend in the trail and saw dozens of lads and lasses about their age. They were walking up the trail to Camp Dragononka.

Right in front of them, a lad sat in the middle of the trail, scraping his boot.

"Torblad!" Wiglaf cried.

Torblad looked up.

"I stepped in something foul," he whined.

A lass stood next to Torblad, handing him leaves. She turned and glanced at Wiglaf.

"I know you," she said. "You slew the dragon Gorzil."

Wiglaf nodded. It had been an accident, but still, he had slain the dragon.

"I am Zelda," said the lass. "I was to be Gorzil's breakfast. You saved my life. Did you get some of Gorzil's golden hoard?"

"No," said Wiglaf.

"Pity," said Zelda. "I took bags of gold from Gorzil's cave."

"Erica! Wiglaf! Angus!" someone cried.

Wiglaf turned and saw Princess Gwendolyn of Gargglethorp running toward them.

"Are you on your way to Camp Dragononka?" asked Gwen.

"Yes!" said Dudwin.

"Excellent!" said Gwen. "I went to Camp Pinecone for Princesses last summer. But this summer, I'm ready for outdoor adventure. Come on! Let's run! I can't wait to get to Camp Dragononka!"

"*This* is camp?" said Angus, peering through a crude wooden gate.

"It sure doesn't look anything like Camp

Pinecone," said Gwen.

Wiglaf swallowed. It was not at all what he had imagined either. He had pictured grassy fields and trees and a big, sparkling blue lake for swimming and boating and healthy, outdoor exercise. He had pictured cozy cabins and smiling counselors.

But what met his eyes was a steep hill. There was no grass, no trees. Only blackened tree stumps poking up from the charred ground. A few flimsy tents. A lake coated with green scum. And next to it, a giant mud puddle. A flagpole stood next to the largest tent. Over it all hung dark gray clouds.

"P.U.! This place stinks!" said Dudwin.

"Maybe it's the stuff on my boot," said Torblad.

"No," said Zelda. "It's the camp." She sniffed the air. "Smells smoky, like burnt shrubbery."

"More like burnt skunk," muttered a big lad. Wiglaf saw that it was Moose, from the Brain Power Tournament.

"Are we supposed to sleep in those tents?" said Gwen.

Janice snapped her gum. "Oh, so what if the camp isn't fancy?" she said. "At least we're all here together. Come on! What are we waiting for?"

And they all ran through the gate into Camp Dragononka.

As they ran, the trill of a whistle split the air. The campers stopped.

Wiglaf looked around. A large man in a bright red tunic and a pair of baggy red shorts was hurrying toward them. A silver whistle hung around his neck.

"Egad!" exclaimed Erica. "He looks exactly like Headmaster Mordred."

"Zounds!" said Wiglaf. "He does."

"Say it's not so!" wailed Angus.

The large man smiled. His gold tooth sparkled in the sunlight.

"Uh-oh," said Janice.

Dudwin broke away from the group and ran toward the man.

"Dudwin, stop!" cried Wiglaf.

But his little brother kept running until he reached the large man.

"Are you Mordred?" Dudwin asked.

"No!" boomed the man.

"Whoa," said Angus. "You could have fooled me."

"Mordred is for school," the man went on. "This is camp. Here I'm known as Mordie." He grinned. "Welcome to Camp Dragononka!"

Chapter 7

"Egad!" cried Angus, staring at his Uncle Mordie. "What's going on?"

Wiglaf was wondering the same thing.

Mordie blew a blast on his silver whistle. *TWEEE!* "Campers! Line up, facing me. Chop chop!"

The campers lined up shoulder to shoulder.

"Good!" boomed Mordie. "I am your camp director. Also the mud wrestling counselor."

"Mordie!" called Moose. "It didn't have mud wrestling on the ad."

"We couldn't put everything on one little

piece of parchment, now could we?" said Mordie. "But this camp has a world-class mud wallow right on the banks of Lake Leechalot."

Lake Leechalot? Wiglaf decided not to sign up for swimming.

"So! Who's ready for supper?" Mordie said. "I'm told that campers will eat anything if you call it by a fun-sounding name."

"He's only fooling, campers!" cried Lady Lobelia as she bolted out of a tent and ran over to her brother. She, too, wore a bright red tunic.

"Call me LoLo," she said. "I'm the Arts and Crafts counselor. I'm sure you are hungry after that hike up to camp. Let's go over to Campfire Circle. And guess what, campers? You get to eat supper outside!"

"Yay!" cried all the campers as LoLo led them over to a stack of smoldering logs.

"Sit down on the ground in a circle around the campfire," said LoLo.

"You call that a campfire?" said Gwen. "At Camp Pinecone, we always had a huge pile of blazing logs."

"Oh, you know how to start a campfire?" asked LoLo eagerly.

"Well, I never actually had to start one myself," muttered Gwen.

"Here, let me do it," said Erica. She knelt beside the smoking logs. By the time all the campers were seated, she had a crackling fire burning.

Wiglaf sat with Dudwin, Daisy, Angus, and Janice. Erica came over and joined them.

Wiglaf looked at everyone sitting around the campfire and his jaw dropped open in surprise. There was Yorick! And Master X! Coach Plungett! And Princess Belcheena!

"Zounds!" he exclaimed. "Half the

teachers from DSA are here!"

"*Iggie-way*," said Daisy, "*I-yay ee-say a-yay oar-bay.*"

"A boar?" Wiglaf looked around. Sure enough, seated between Coach Plungett and Princess Belcheena was a large and bristly boar. He had gold-tipped tusks that shone in the firelight. "I remember him. He came to DSA with Princess Belcheena."

Daisy nodded as she stared across the campfire at the boar. "*E-hay is-yay ery-vay andsome-hay.*"

Mordie planted a camp stool beside the campfire and sat down.

"Counselors?" he said. "Stand and tell your camp nicknames."

"Wait!" cried Gwen.

Mordie glared at her. "For what?"

"At Camp Pinecone," she said, "we always started campfire with the camp song."

"Uh—uh, well, this is Camp Dragononka," sputtered Mordie. "And we don't need a camp song."

"But Mordie," said LoLo. "I wrote one." She stepped close to the campfire. "I'll sing it first, campers. Then you join in." And she sang:

> "Hail! Hail! Camp Dragononka!
> We pledge ourselves to thee!
> There's no camp like Dragononka,
> With its stumps of trees!
> In Lake Leechalot you'll paddle,
> Hike on Ridgetop Trail!
> Outdoor fun for lads and lasses.
> Dragononka, hail!"

Wiglaf sang along with the other campers. The smoky smell was even stronger now. His eyes were watering. They burned. Even though he had never been to camp before, he knew there was something not quite right about Camp Dragononka.

After the song, the counselors stood and said their nicknames.

Coach Plungett shouted, "Plungie!"

Princess Belcheena said, "Belchie! And this is my boar, Tusker."

"*Usker-tay,*" Daisy sighed.

Master X stood. As always, the former executioner's head was completely covered by a black hood. "Call me Axe Man," he said.

Yorick stood and said, "YoRick!"

Frypot stood. "Call me Cookie," he said.

"Thank you, counselors," said Mordie. "Now, campers, it's fee time!" His violet eyes gleamed with joy. "Get out those three shiny pennies! YoRick will collect them."

YoRick shook out a bag and began walking from camper to camper.

"Three pennies," she said, stopping in front of Dudwin.

Dudwin plunked in his three pennies.

YoRick moved on to Wiglaf. "Three pennies," he said.

"He brought three friends, Yo," Dudwin said. "Erica, Angus, and Janice. They paid."

"So I get in for free," said Wiglaf.

"Free?" Mordie cried racing toward Wiglaf. "Did somebody say 'free'?"

"I did," said Wiglaf.

"You! I might have known!" Mordie boomed.

Wiglaf's hand shook as he held up the parchment. He pointed to the extra-small print.

Mordie read it, his violet eyes sizzling.

"What maggot-brained fool wrote *this*?" Mordie bellowed, waving the parchment. "I'll put whoever did it in the thumb screws!"

LoLo rushed over. "You wrote it, Mordie."

"Impossible!" cried Mordie.

"You said it was a brilliant sales pitch," LoLo reminded him.

"Free? I've never written that word in my life," Mordie mumbled as LoLo took his arm and pulled him back to his camp stool. "Never!"

Chapter 8

ow it was Cookie's turn to walk around the Campfire Circle. He handed each camper a stick with a white, jelly-like blob stuck on the pointed end.

"Here ye go." He handed one to Wiglaf.

"What is this?" asked Wiglaf.

"I call it supper-on-a-stick," said Cookie. "Roast it well, just to be on the safe side."

Wiglaf and the other campers held their sticks over the fire. A foul, fishy odor filled the air, mixing with the smoky smell. Wiglaf took a bite. Gack! Whatever it was tasted worse than the eel they ate back at DSA. Much worse!

Mordie stood up. "Camp Dragononka is a special place," he said. "You can make doo-dads in Arts and Crafts. You can win relay races. You can take a plunge in Lake Leechalot. You can make new friends. Or maybe you won't. I was never good at making friends myself, when I was a lad. And look how marvelously I turned out."

As Mordie talked on and on, Daisy leaned over to Wiglaf.

"*I-yay am-yay oing-gay o-tay ed-bay,*" she whispered.

"Where will you sleep?" asked Wiglaf.

"*I-yay all-shay ind-fay a-yay ot-spay,*" she said, and she trotted off.

"You'll be out in the fresh air all day, hiking and digging," Mordie was saying.

Dudwin leaned toward Wiglaf. "It didn't say anything about digging on the ad, did it?"

Wiglaf shook his head. Digging did not

sound like a camp activity.

"At the end of camp, two teams will compete in the BIG DIG!" Mordie grinned. "More on that later. Each member of the winning team will get a valuable prize!" He held up a small red patch with an upside-down dragon on it.

"*That's* the valuable prize?" Angus whispered.

"Campfire's over for tonight," Mordie said. "Campers? Off for bed."

"Wait!" called Gwen.

Mordred's eyes sizzled. "Now what?"

"At Camp Pinecone," she said, "campfire always ended with a ghost story."

"We want a ghost story!" cried Dudwin. "We want a ghost story!"

Other campers picked up the chant.

"Too bad," said Mordie. "I don't know any ghost stories."

"I do," said Axe Man, his voice slightly muffled by his hood. He rose slowly to his feet.

A shiver went up Wiglaf's spine.

"Some of you may be wondering why I wear this black hood over my head," Axe Man said. "I wonder myself at times. Gets bloody hot under here in the summer."

Axe Man paused. Wiglaf wondered if under his hood, he was smiling.

"I shall tell you why I wear this hood," Axe Man went on. "I was once an executioner. My job was to whack the heads off of thieves, robbers, murderers, poisoners, and plotters against the king." He lifted an imaginary axe and brought it swiftly down. "Whacko!"

All the campers jumped in their seats.

"In days gone by, King Richard the Ferret-Hearted ruled the land," Axe Man said. "He was a good king. Only a little disorganized. One day King Richard called me to him.

"'Master X,' he said, for so I was called, 'Master X, tonight my guards will bring a prisoner to Bloody Hill. I want you to go there, and at the stroke of midnight, whack off his head.'

"'Good as done, your highness,' I said. 'Might I ask who this prisoner is?'

"'The Duke of Devormore,' said the king.

"I gasped! For ever since I was a teeny-tiny lad, I had heard tales of this cruel Duke. Mothers all over the realm told their children to be good, or the Duke of Devormore would come and get them. Oh! Some of the things he did would make your toes curl. How proud I felt when I heard that I would be the one to execute him. Yet part of me had a bad feeling about this job. Bloody Hill is not a place to be at midnight, even for an axe-wielding executioner."

Wiglaf shivered.

"I sharpened the blade of my axe," Axe
Man went on. "Washed and ironed my hood.
Then I set off for Bloody Hill. It was a long
walk. There was no moon that night, nor
stars, either. But I have eyes like a cat, and
can see in the dark, and well I knew the
way. When I reached the top of Bloody Hill,
I spied two guards standing beside a tree
stump. Between them, they held the Duke.
He wore a dark cape around his shoulders
and he was deathly pale. As I approached, he
laughed: 'Whoohaaaaahaaaaahaaaaa!'"

Wiglaf and the other campers jumped.

"My victims generally do not laugh
when they see me coming," Axe Man said.
"But the Duke could not stop laughing:
'Whoohaaaaahaaaaahaaaaa!'

"I didn't like his laughter," Axe Man went

on. "I wanted to whack off his head and be done with it. So I told the guards to fold back the collar of the Duke's cape so I could see his neck. And to place the Duke's neck on the tree stump. They did as I asked. But even when he was face down, with his lily-white neck on the stump, the Duke laughed: 'Whoohaaaaahaaaaahaaaaa!'

"Keeping my eyes on his neck, I raised my axe, and brought it down: WHACK! What did I hear? Was it the sound of a head hitting the ground? Not this time. No, what I heard was: 'Whoohaaaaahaaaaahaaaaa!'"

Some of the campers squealed. Wiglaf and his friends huddled closer together.

"At the sound of the Duke's laughter, the guards ran screaming into the night," said Axe Man. "I looked down at my axe blade. It was sunk deep in the tree stump. On one side of my axe blade, I saw the Duke's body. On the other side of my blade, I saw his head. I had chopped clean through the Duke's neck, but his head was still attached to his body.

"The Duke sprang up before my eyes. His flesh melted away until all that was left were his bones. He opened his jaw bone and laughed: 'Whoohaaaaahaaaaahaaaaa!' Then he shouted, 'The Duke of Devormore has been dead for fifty years! Don't you know you can't execute a ghost?'"

Torblad began to whimper.

"Then the ghostly white skin began to appear on the bones once more," Axe Man went on. "The Duke swirled his cape around him. I heard him laughing as he floated off over Bloody Hill: 'Whoohaaaaahaaaaahaaaaa!'"

All the campers huddled together in bunches, so as not to be scared. The campfire had burned down to embers now.

"The next day, I retired," Axe Man said. "I became an ex-executioner. But I still wear this hood to remind myself of the night when I couldn't whack the head off a ghost."

Axe Man threw back his head and laughed. "Whoohaaaaahaaaaahaaaaa!"

And all the campers screamed and screamed.

Chapter 9

fter campfire, Plungie led Wiglaf and the other lads to their tent.

Wiglaf, still shivering from the scary story, leaned toward his brother. "You can sleep next to me if you are frightened, Dud," he said.

"I love ghost stories!" said Dudwin. "The scarier the better."

They ducked into the lads' tent.

"Hey, where are the cots?" said Angus.

"Cots are for dorms," said Plungie. "You're at camp now. You get to sleep on the ground!"

Dudwin lay down. Wiglaf spread the

warm royal blue blanket over him.

"Good night, Wiggie," said Dudwin. "Thank you for bringing me to camp."

"Sleep well, Dud," said Wiglaf. He rolled up in his thin brown blanket and closed his eyes. It was quiet in the lads' tent.

Except for Angus, muttering "cream puffs, cream puffs" softly in his sleep.

Suddenly horrible laughter rang out: "Whoohaaaaahaaaaahaaaaa!"

All the lads jumped up, shrieking.

Except for Dudwin, who was rolling around on the ground, laughing.

"Dudwin, was that you?" said Wiglaf.

Dudwin did not answer. He kept on laughing like a maniac. "Scared you guys, didn't I?"

"Yes!" whimpered Torblad.

The lads settled in once more. But Wiglaf could not fall asleep. He worried that

Dudwin would try to scare them all again. He heard what sounded like wolves howling in the woods. And the flapping wings of some large bird. He could not get the Duke of Devormore out of his head. Where was Bloody Hill, anyway? Was it anywhere near Dragononka Ridge?

At last Wiglaf threw off his blanket. Counting stars always made him sleepy, so he snuck quietly out of the tent. He sat down on the ground. He gazed up at the sky. But thick, billowy clouds covered the stars.

After a while, Daisy trotted by.

"*I-yay ouldn't-cay eep-slay,*" she said, sitting down beside him.

"Me either," said Wiglaf, feeling safer with his pig at his side. He turned and looked toward the top of Dragononka Ridge. It, too, was hidden by clouds. Then, as he watched, the billowy clouds blew away. Lightning flashed. And in that flash, Wiglaf saw that the ridge was lined with huge, jagged stones.

"Look, Daisy," said Wiglaf. "Those stones! They make the top of Dragononka Ridge look exactly like the spiky back of a dragon!"

Toot-toot tooty-toot TOOT.

The bugle's blast woke Wiglaf.

"Up and at 'em, lads!" Plungie called from somewhere outside the lads' tent.

Wiglaf heard campers calling, "Look! In the sky! What does it mean?"

Wiglaf scrambled out of his blanket and ran out of the tent. He looked up. Dark billowy clouds had taken the shapes of letters that spelled out:

S C R A M

Suddenly, Dudwin was at his side.

"What's it say, Wiggie?" he asked.

"SCRAM," said Wiglaf.

"'Tis an omen!" wailed Torblad, nearly in tears. "Something bad shall happen!"

Mordie came tromping toward the tents. LoLo was right behind him.

"Nothing to worry about, campers!" Mordie boomed. "We get clouds in all sorts of shapes and sizes here. That's part of what makes Camp Dragononka so special. All right, line up for the Camp Dragononka flag-raising."

The campers stood silently while YoRick raised a red flag with an upside-down dragon on it to the top of the flagpole.

"Repeat after me!" said Mordie. He put a hand to his heart and said:

"Whatever I say and whatever I do,

To Camp Dragononka I shall be—"

He stopped. "No, no," he said. He thought for a moment. Then said, "Here we go.

"To Camp Dragononka. I shall be true,
And do what Mordie says I should do!"
Mordie grinned. "Say it with me!"
The campers did.

"Breakfast is ready!" called LoLo.

On his way to Campfire Circle, Wiglaf
looked around for Daisy but didn't see her.

Cookie was handing out sticks again.

"What's this?" cried Dudwin, looking at
the gristly blob stuck to the end of his stick.

"I call it breakfast-on-a-stick," said Cookie.
"Roast it good and eat up!"

When the campers had finished nibbling at
whatever it was on their sticks, Mordie said,
"Come on, campers! Let's go on a hike!"

"You mean a *nature* hike, don't you,
Mordie?" said Gwen. "At Camp Pinecone, we
went on nature hikes all the time. We looked
at rocks and plants and animal tracks."

"Whatever you call it," said Mordie. "You

campers need to learn your way to the top of Dragononka Ridge. Line up! Chop chop!"

The campers lined up under the cloudy sky. LoLo started them off singing:

"Hail! Hail! Camp Dragononka!

We pledge ourselves to thee!"

They marched out of the charred campgrounds and up Ridgetop Trail. Wiglaf's eyes began to burn. They felt even worse than they had the night before.

As he hiked up the trail, Wiglaf looked down and saw Daisy and Tusker lolling in the mud wallow. He smiled. His pig had made a friend!

The trail was hard-packed dirt and rock.

"There's a branberry bush," said Gwen, pointing to a shrub at the side of the trail.

"So it is," said Mordie.

"And look!" said Gwen. "Here is a rare whistledown thistle."

"A fine example, too," said Mordie.

Wiglaf began to wonder how much Mordie really knew about nature.

"Stop!" cried Erica suddenly. "Tracks!"

She knelt down to examine them.

Wiglaf saw a set of footprints embedded in the rocky trail. Huge footprints! Each print had three long toes. At the tip of each toe was a round hole.

"What tracks are these, sir?" asked Torblad, his voice trembling.

"Sir is for school!" Mordie boomed. "This is camp. Call me Mordie!"

"What tracks are these, Mordie?" said Torblad, his voice still trembling.

"Uh...why...rabbit tracks," said Mordie.

"They are dragon tracks," said Erica.

"Dragon, schmagon," said Mordie quickly. "All right. Onward and upward!"

"Pick up any pretty little stones you

see," LoLo told the campers as they hiked. "We'll use them to make jewelry in Arts and Crafts."

Most of the stones on the trail were black and shiny, as if they had been burned in a fire. Wiglaf did not pick up any stones until he spotted a blue one. He picked it up.

Dudwin picked up nearly every stone he saw. Soon his pockets were bulging.

As she hiked, Erica unhooked a small book from her tool belt. She flipped it to a picture and handed the book to Wiglaf. He looked at the drawing of a three-toed footprint much like the ones on the trail. Under the picture were the words: "Dragon track." Wiglaf handed the book to Angus.

"There's something fishy about this camp," said Angus, handing the book to Janice.

"The food?" said Janice, snapping her gum.

"More than that," said Angus. "I know Uncle Mordie. There's something he isn't telling us."

Ridgetop Trail grew steeper and steeper. Most of the campers had to stop to catch their breath. And all the campers complained that their eyes stung. Dudwin was carrying so many stones in his pockets that for once, he did not race ahead.

"Good...thing...I...have...been...jogging," Angus panted as he climbed. "Or...I'd... never...make...it."

As they climbed higher, the air grew foggy and even more foul-smelling.

All the campers started coughing.

"It stinks up here!" cried Dudwin.

"My eyes are burning," said Erica.

"My gum tastes awful!" said Janice, and she spit it out.

Still, on they went. Soon, there was so

much fog on the ground that Wiglaf could not see his own boots.

At last they stopped. Wiglaf saw huge jagged stones sticking up through the fog—the stones he had seen the night before when the lightning flashed. There were dozens of them.

"C-c-campers!" coughed Mordie. "Congratulations! You've made it all the way to the top of Dragononka Ridge."

"Yay!" cheered the campers. Then they coughed some more.

"You'll be hiking this trail every morning," Mordie added.

"Nooooo!" wailed the campers.

"Yes!" said Mordie. "Soon you'll be running up here in no time. And you'll be digging great big holes to find—to find—er, nature stuff."

Wiglaf frowned. Why was Mordie always

talking about digging?

"Mordie!" called out Moose. "What are those giant stones?"

"Who knows?" said Mordie. "But they're part of what makes Camp Dragononka so special."

"Brrrr!" Janice shivered, but not from the cold. "This place gives me the creeps."

"You, too?" said Wiglaf, surprised. Janice was always such a good sport about everything.

"Whoohaaaaahaaaaahaaaaa!" Dudwin laughed insanely again.

Torblad shrieked.

"Cut it out, Dud," said Wiglaf. He pinched his nose to stop the horrid smell.

"I think those stones look like statues," said Erica.

"Yeah, ancient ones," said Janice. "Like they've been standing up here for hundreds of years and gotten worn down from rains and wind."

Wiglaf nodded. That was exactly what they looked like.

"Mordie?" It was Moose again. "I heard an old legend about this place."

"Legend, schmegend," said Mordie. "Don't believe everything you hear. All right, campers! What goes up must come down!"

He and LoLo led the campers back down the ridge. With every step, the stink faded.

About halfway down, Dudwin wandered off the trail.

"Dud!" called Wiglaf, hurrying after him. "Come back!" What was his little brother up to now?

Wiglaf found Dudwin on his knees, with a stick in his hand. He was trying to loosen something stuck in a gnarled tree root.

"Dud, you have enough rocks," said

Wiglaf. "You don't have to get this one."

"Not a rock," said Dudwin.

Wiglaf peered at the thing Dudwin was prying out. It was long and white and curved. It ended in a sharp point.

"Zounds!" he cried. "What is that?"

Dudwin pressed on his stick and suddenly the thing popped out from the root. It landed a few feet away on the trail. It was a fang.

Wiglaf and Dudwin stared at the fang. It had a dark hole through the middle. It reminded Wiglaf of the dragon Seetha's rotten teeth.

Dudwin snatched the thing up and held it in his fist. "Whooie! Guess who found a dragon fang?"

"You did, Dud," said Wiglaf. "Now let's go."

"Wait!" cried Dudwin. "There are more

fangs under this root. Lots more!"

Dudwin kept digging until he'd unearthed a dozen rotten, holey fangs. Only then could Wiglaf persuade him to walk back down to camp.

My Darling Poopsie Pie,

Lady Thinwisp's Slimming Center was simply dreadful! Lady T's idea of soup is lukewarm barley water. Radishia and I lasted for two days and then came home. From now on, I'll eat what I like and enjoy it, and I hope you'll do the same!

Angus, I know you are getting lots of outdoor exercise. So here is a special treat — a great big box of Medieval Marshmallows for you to toast over the campfire. Be sure to share them with your fellow campers, Poopsie!

Love and kisses,
Mother

Chapter 10

Wiglaf had been at Camp Dragononka for three days. He was getting used to the dark, cloudy sky. The awful smell. The coughing. The daily hikes. Even the meals-on-a-stick. But he could not get used to the strange howling and flapping sounds he heard in the dark. He hadn't had a good night's sleep since he'd been at camp.

"What makes that flapping noise every night, Mordie?" Wiglaf asked one morning as he and the other campers were roasting their breakfasts-on-a-stick.

"It's just the wind," said Mordie. "One more thing that makes this camp so..."

"Special," Wiglaf muttered to himself. *Weird* was more like it.

After breakfast, he and several other campers sat down on the picnic cloth that LoLo called the Arts and Crafts area. They watched as LoLo took a shiny black stone and tied two thin leather strips around it.

"See?" She held up the stone bound by the strips. "Now I'll tie a few knots in the leather..." She did so. "And now I'll tie in another stone." Before long, LoLo had a bracelet.

"Cool!" said Janice, sounding more like her usual self. "I'm going to make my mom a bracelet just like that."

"Me too," said Erica. She dumped all the black stones she had collected onto the cloth. "Although I don't know why she would wear a common rock bracelet when she has so many jewels."

Wiglaf took the blue stone from his pocket.

He liked the way it shone. He hoped Molwena would like it. She had no jewelry, so she would not object to wearing a rock bracelet. He took two leather strips and began tying them in knots.

"Look what I made!" cried Dudwin. "A fang necklace!" He held up a leather strip that he'd threaded through the cavities in the fangs. Grinning, he put the necklace around his neck. "How do I look, Wiggie?"

"It suits you, Dud," Wiglaf said. He was glad that his little brother was busy. And not trying to scare everybody.

"What are you making, Wiggie?" asked Dudwin.

"A bracelet for our mother," said Wiglaf. "It can be from both of us."

"Nah," said Dudwin. "I'll make her something later."

After Arts and Crafts, Wiglaf went

searching for Daisy. He found her and Tusker sitting on the shore of Lake Leechalot.

"*Ello-hay, Iggie-way,*" said Daisy.

"I have been missing you, Daisy," Wiglaf said. "Are you having fun?"

"*Es-yay.*" Daisy smiled. She told him that she liked lolling in the mud with Tusker. "*E-hay is-yay o-say ood-gay ooking-lay.*" She sighed. "*If-yay only-yay e-hay ould-cay alk-tay!*"

"Perhaps I should summon Zelnoc," said Wiglaf. "He could put a speech spell on Tusker."

Daisy's eyes grew wide. "*Es-yay! O-day at-thay!*"

But the lunch gong rang, so Wiglaf had to hurry to the campfire. He sat down with the other campers, picking at their lunches-on-a-stick.

"What is this stuff?" asked Zelda.

"Best you don't know, lass," said Cookie.

"Trust me on this."

Mordie strode over to the campfire.
"Today is a special day, campers," he said. "It's
the day you find out what Dragon team you're
on." He pointed to Torblad. "Count off by
twos!"

"Two!" shouted Torblad.

Mordie's violet eyes bulged. "Start
counting with *one*."

"One," sniveled Torblad, who hated to be
yelled at.

"Two!" called Moose.

"One!" called Angus.

"Two!" called Dudwin. "Hey, Moose! I'm
on your team!"

"Shush!" said Mordie. "Count!"

"One!" called Wiglaf.

"Two!" called Zelda.

The counting continued until every
camper was either a one or a two.

"Ones? You're Cave Dragons," said Mordie. "Twos? You're Swamp Dragons."

Cave Dragon—Wiglaf liked the sound of it. Erica and Angus were Cave Dragons. So were Janice and Gwen. But Dudwin was a Swamp Dragon.

"From now on you'll sit with your teammates," said Mordie. "Cave Dragons sit on this side of the fire." Mordie pointed. "Swamp Dragons, on the other side."

"Dudwin, behave yourself..." Wiglaf warned.

But Dudwin wasn't listening. He darted over to the Swamp Dragons. He started cackling and waggling his fingers as if they were claws. "I'm a mean, green Swamp Dragon!" he cried. "I'm coming to eat up every Cave Dragon I can find." He gave a terrible roar.

"Stop that!" cried Torblad.

"Who wants to be captain of the Swamp

Dragons?" said Mordie.

"Me! Me! Me!" called Dudwin.

"I want to be captain," said Zelda. "How much will it cost me, Mordie?"

Mordie's violet eyes lit up. "Oh! A lass after my own heart!" he squealed. "I appoint you captain. See me after breakfast."

"Hey!" cried Dudwin. "That's not fair."

"Shush," said Mordie. "All right, who wants to be captain of the Cave Dragons?"

"Me!" yelled Erica and Gwen at the same time.

"Well?" said Mordie. "Make me an offer."

"At Camp Pinecone, we voted for captain," said Gwen.

"Good idea," said Erica. "Vote for me. I've already made up a Cave Dragon cheer." She yelled:

"We are the Cave Dragons!

We're number one!
You can try to beat us,
But it can't be done!"

All the Cave Dragons cheered.

Gwen rolled her eyes and said, "Vote for me, Cave Dragons. I've been to camp before. I know all there is to know about winning."

Mordie had the Cave Dragons close their eyes and raise their hands. He counted the votes.

"Open your eyes," he said. "Gwen wins."

"WHAT?" cried Erica.

"Shush," said Mordie.

For the next few days, Erica was not herself. She never cheered once during the Rocks-in-the-Backpack relay races. She dug the smallest hole in Speed Digging. In Swimming, she even refused to put her toe into Lake Leechalot.

"I don't like green ooze," she said.

One morning as she and Wiglaf hiked up to the top of Dragononka Ridge, she said, "I still can't believe I lost the election. I'm always captain of everything!"

"If there is a Best Camper of the Month medal, you shall win that," said Wiglaf.

Erica brightened. "Do you think so?"

That night on the way to campfire, Wiglaf spied Dudwin walking with Moose. He had not seen much of his brother since he became a Swamp Dragon. He caught up with him.

"Sit by me at campfire," said Wiglaf.

"No! You are a Cave Dragon and my enemy!" Dudwin started cackling again.

"Cut it out, Dud," said Wiglaf. "Just sit by me this one time."

"I am a prisoner of the Cave Dragons!" Dudwin called as he sat down next to his brother.

"Hey, Mordie?" Moose called when all the campers were seated. "When do we get to toast marshmallows over a roaring fire like it said in the ad?"

"Yes!" called all the campers. "When?"

"Oh, other camps roast marshmallows all the time," said Mordie. "But here at Camp Dragononka, we have a special Marshmallow Roasting Night."

"In other words, he's saying we get to roast marshmallows only once," whispered Angus. Wiglaf glanced at his friend. He had seen the marshmallow-filled goodie box hidden under his bedroll. But Angus had not offered to share.

Tonight was Torblad's turn to tell a ghost story. It was a long tale about a haunted cheese shop in Toenail.

As Torblad talked on and on, Dudwin began staring into the fire.

A moment later, he gave a start and grabbed Wiglaf's arm.

"I see a ghost, Wiggie!" Dudwin whispered. "A dragon ghost!"

"Cut it out, Dud," said Wiglaf.

"I'm not fooling!" Dudwin whispered. "It's in the flames of the fire."

"Quiet over there!" called Torblad. "You're wrecking my ghost story!"

"Sorry," muttered Wiglaf.

"Oh, it's gone now," Dudwin whispered.

"Flames can take on strange shapes, Dud," said Wiglaf, keeping his voice low. "They can make you think you see things that are not there."

"It was there," whispered Dudwin. "Floating over the flames. I saw it!" He glanced at his brother. "You don't believe me, do you, Wiggie?"

Dear Ma and Pa,

I hope the village postal peasant will read you this letter.

Dudwin and Daisy and I are all at Camp Dragononka. Every day we hike and dig holes and run relay races carrying heavy rocks in our packs. It is not what I thought I might do at camp. But I am growing strong!

I am making you a bracelet in Arts and Crafts, Ma. It has a shiny blue stone. I hope you will like it.

Your son,

Wiglaf

Chapter 11

"**W**ood chopping can be fun!" said Axe
Man as the campers lined up in front of him.
They watched the hooded counselor test the
sharpness of his axe blade by running his
fingers down it.

"Nice and sharp!" he said as blood
spurted from his thumb.

Wiglaf gagged. Why couldn't Axe Man
have tested his axe on a log?

"All these logs need to be chopped into
firewood," Axe Man told the campers.
"Here's how you do it. Stand a log on end
on a flat stump. Then—WHACKO!" He
chopped the log in two. "See? Do like I do

and pretend you're whacking off a head."

Axe Man passed out small axes.

Dudwin ran off to chop wood with
Moose.

"Be careful, Dudwin," Wiglaf called after
him. Then he and Angus picked up their logs
and went off to find a flat stump.

"This place smells disgusting," said Angus
as he put his log on the charred stump.
"The sun never shines. I wonder why Uncle
Mordie opened a camp here."

Axe Man came by to check on them.

"Hold the axe handle with both hands,"
he told Angus. "Then—whammo!"

Angus and Wiglaf tried it. But they only
succeeded in knocking the log off the stump.

"Oh, never mind," said Axe Man at last.
"You lads can gather kindling."

"Axe Man?" said Wiglaf. "What do you
know about Dragononka Ridge?"

"There's an old legend about a burial ground on top of the ridge," said Axe Man.

Wiglaf remembered Moose saying something about a legend.

"Who is buried up there?" asked Wiglaf.

"The legend says it's dragons." Axe Man turned and gazed up at the fog-covered peak. "And that their ghosts live up there still."

"Dragon ghosts?" cried Wiglaf.

Axe Man laughed. "'Tis only a legend, lads," he said. "Just leave your axe stuck in the stump when you go to look for kindling." And he moved on.

"Dudwin said he saw a dragon ghost floating over the campfire last night," Wiglaf told Angus.

Angus shrugged. "He's probably heard the old legend, too. He was trying to scare you."

Wiglaf nodded. That was it. Dudwin was

just trying to scare him.

Angus grabbed hold of the axe handle. He swung the axe back, ready to thunk it down onto the stump. Instead, his axe stayed where it was, behind his back. Angus looked like a frozen statue.

"Angus!" cried Wiglaf. "What's wrong?"

"I—I don't know, Wiggie!" Angus cried. "I can't move the axe. It's like something is holding on to it."

A moment later, Angus brought the axe down into the stump. He jumped back from it. "That was weird!" he said. "Maybe I had a muscle cramp."

Later, when Wiglaf and Angus went back to the tent, they discovered something even weirder.

"Ugh!" cried Wiglaf when he lifted the tent flap. "It stinks in there!"

"Gadzooks!" cried Angus. "Look!"

The bedrolls and blankets were bunched in a heap and covered in slime.

"Oh, no!" cried Angus. "Where's my..." He raced inside.

Wiglaf heard a scream.

And Angus reappeared at the tent flap. "My goodie box! Empty!" he cried. "And there's cold, slimy, stinky goo all over it!"

Angus squeezed his eyes shut, fighting back tears. "Who would do such a deed?"

Wiglaf shook his head. He only hoped it wasn't Dudwin.

Over the next few cloudy days, Angus questioned everyone about his missing marshmallows. And the slimy box. Soon rumors began flying—Camp Dragononka was haunted!

"Camp Dragononka is NOT haunted,"

Mordie announced a few mornings later at breakfast.

"Yes, it is!" cried Dudwin.

"Shush!" said Mordie.

Torblad began to snivel.

"Is this camp foggy?" said Mordie. "Yes. Windy at night? Yes. And because of the fog and the wind, some fool made up a legend about the ghosts of Dragononka Ridge."

"Tell it to us!" cried a camper.

"Tonight at campfire, LoLo shall tell you the legend," Mordie said.

"I shall?" said LoLo, surprised.

"You shall," said Mordie.

As always, clouds hid the moon as the campers sat down around Campfire Circle that night. Some of the younger lads and lasses had brought along their teddy bears in case the legend was very scary.

LoLo stood up. "Um..." she said. "Long, long ago, there lived a dragon."

The little campers hugged their bears.

"The dragon's name was Fifi," LoLo went on. "She was polite and friendly and very pretty. But she was lonely."

"This isn't a ghost story!" cried Dudwin.

"Shush!" called Mordie from his camp stool.

"So one day Fifi invited all the dragons she knew to a party on top of Dragononka Ridge," LoLo went on. "She hired a band to play beautiful music."

Wiglaf saw that the young campers had stopped squeezing their teddy bears.

"Fifi greeted her guests wearing a gown of pink rose petals," LoLo said. "On her head, she wore a pointed pink rose petal hat."

"Where are the ghosts?" Janice called.

"Ghosts," said LoLo. "I almost forgot. Well, the band began to play and the dragons danced all night long. When dawn came, the dragons kept dancing. They danced for days. The days turned into weeks, and the weeks turned into months, and the months turned into years. And still they danced."

A loud snore sounded. Wiglaf saw that Mordie had fallen sound asleep. He was tilting dangerously on his camp stool.

"On and on the dragons danced," LoLo shouted over Mordie's snores, "until one by one, they dropped dead of old age. And now their ghosts live up on top of Dragononka Ridge. And sometimes, if the clouds lift, you might think you see the ghosts of Fifi and her friends, dancing."

After campfire, Wiglaf and Angus caught

up with Dudwin. They walked together to the lads' tent.

"That wasn't the real legend," said Angus.

"No way," said Dudwin. "Anyway, dragon ghosts never have names like Fifi. They have dragony names like Gringador and Pitgasher."

"How do you know, Dud?" asked Wiglaf.

"I just do," said Dudwin.

In the middle of the night, Wiglaf felt someone shaking him. He opened his eyes.

"Wiggie," whispered Dudwin. "The ghosts are here. See for yourself."

Wiglaf groaned. "No more jokes, Dud."

"This isn't a joke," said Dudwin. "I swear."

Wiglaf slipped out from under his blanket. He and Dudwin crept out of the tent.

"Look," said Dudwin. "They're everywhere."

"I don't see any ghosts," said Wiglaf.

Dudwin grabbed Wiglaf's hand and half pulled him up the hill.

"There," said Dudwin.

"I still don't see any—" Wiglaf stopped.

Near the flagpole, he saw big rocks that seemed to be floating through the air.

"R-rocks," Wiglaf managed.

"The ghosts are bringing them," said Dudwin.

Wiglaf stared. One by one, the rocks floated out of the woods and fell to the ground near the flagpole.

"We must tell Mordie," Wiglaf said.

They ran to Mordie's tent.

"Sir?" Wiglaf cried.

"Sir is for school!" Mordie called sleepily from inside the tent. "This is camp. Go away!"

"Emergency, Mordie!" called Wiglaf.

"Be gone!" cried Mordie.

"Ghosts!" cried Dudwin.

Mordie poked his face out through the tent flap.

"Ghosts, schmosts," he said. "I'll give you to the count of ten to get back to your tent or I'll set the hounds on you. One!"

"What hounds?" said Dudwin.

"Two!" growled Mordie.

"You don't have any hounds," said Dudwin.

"Three!" called Mordie. "Four! Five! Six!"

"Come on, Dudwin!" cried Wiglaf, yanking at his brother's tunic. The lads turned and ran as fast as they could down the hill. All Wiglaf wanted was to be safe inside the tent, under his blanket, away from the floating rocks.

Hey, Mom! Hey, Dad!

How are you? Is the house finished, Mom? How is your statue coming, Dad? Is Aunt Gert still there? Has Bibs stopped biting?

I LOVE camp! We have teams here. I am on the Cave Dragons team. We rock! We compete against the Swamp Dragons in all sorts of sports—rock-toting relays, hole digging, weight lifting, wood chopping, and swimming. Lake Leechalot is covered with scum, but once you dive in it's not too bad.

Perchance, could you send me a few more packs of gum?

I miss you!

Love,

Janice

Chapter 12

Wiglaf was jolted awake the next morning by Torblad yelling from outside the tent. "Alas! Doom is upon us!"

Wiglaf sprang up and ran out of the tent. Dudwin was right behind him. He looked up in the sky to see if there was another message, but saw only thick, dark clouds.

"What is going on?" he asked Janice, who had just come out of the lasses' tent.

"I know not," Janice said. "Let's go see."

A crowd had gathered near the flagpole. They were looking up the hill. When Wiglaf got there, he saw what everyone was staring at. Big rocks spelled out:

GO AWAY

"What's it say, Wiggie?" cried Dudwin.

"Go away," said Wiglaf.

"G-O," said Dudwin. "That spells 'go'?"

Wiglaf nodded.

"The ghosts are trying to get us to G-O, go," said Dudwin. "They put those rocks there to send us a message! You believe me now, don't you, Wiggie?"

Just then Torblad ran past them, yelling, "I'm going home to Toenail!"

"Nobody's going home!" boomed Mordred.

"Mordie?" said Zelda. "Why do the rocks say GO AWAY?"

"Why, it's part of that old rhyme," said Mordie. "Rain, rain, go away. It means we'll have sunshine today! I'll bet your friends at other camps don't get to wake up and find fun, mysterious rock messages. No, sir. That only happens at Camp Dragononka!"

That afternoon, the Cave Dragons went up against the Swamp Dragons in the Rock-a-Thon relay race.

"Here's the drill," Plungie said when all the campers had gathered at the flagpole. "When I say GO, you run and pick up a sack and a shovel and start digging! Dig up three rocks and toss them into your sacks. Then run to the next person on your team and hand off the sack and the shovel."

Wiglaf's head was spinning. He had a hard time listening to Plungie's directions. Was their camp haunted? Or was Dudwin playing tricks on him again?

"Ready?" Plungie shouted.

"Swamp Dragons are ready!" cried Zelda.

"Cave Dragons are ready!" yelled Gwen.

Plungie cried, "Go!"

Erica and a Swamp Dragon took off running and picked up the shovels. Once they started digging, Erica quickly came up with three good-sized rocks. She tossed them into the sack and ran back to the Cave Dragons. She handed the sack and the shovel to Gwen, who took off running.

Wiglaf watched as Gwen dug. Now she was running toward him. He was next! She passed him the sack. It was heavy, but he swung it onto his back and ran to the hole. He started digging. He heard a Swamp Dragon beside him, digging, too. Wiglaf dug up one rock, two rocks, three. He threw them into the sack. He could hardly lift the thing, but he managed to stagger back to his team. Janice was waiting. She grabbed the sack and the shovel and took off running.

Moose from the Swamp Dragons was right beside her. He and Janice dug furiously. They threw the rocks into their sacks and sped for the finish line. At the last moment, Janice put on a burst of speed and crossed the line just ahead of Moose.

"Hooray, Cave Dragons!" cried Erica.

Everyone on the team cheered.

But when the cheering died down, Gwen shook her head. "We never did stuff like this at Camp Pinecone," she muttered.

That night at campfire, Mordie announced the Dragon team scores.

"The Swamp Dragons and Cave Dragons are tied, with 510 points each." He smiled. "Close race. Looks like the Big Dig will decide the winner."

"Swampy, Swampy, Swampy!" cheered the Swamp Dragons. "We're gonna swamp you!"

Erica jumped to her feet and led her

favorite cheer:

"Cave Dragons rule!
That's no jest!
Cave Dragons! Cave Dragons!
We're the best!"

"Yay!" cried all the Cave Dragons.

"Mordie?" called Moose. "When do we get to hear about the BIG DIG?"

Mordie grinned. "Very soon," he said.

Now LoLo stood. "Who would like to tell tonight's ghost story?" she said. "Someone who hasn't had a turn yet."

To Wiglaf's surprise, Dudwin jumped up and walked up to stand beside LoLo.

"Me," he said.

"All right, Dudwin," said LoLo. "Begin."

"I see ghosts—dragon ghosts," said Dudwin in a creepy voice. "I see them every night now."

"Nooooo!" called out some campers.

"I do," said Dudwin. He took hold of his fang necklace. "I saw one right here, floating over the campfire."

"Oooooh!" cried a few campers.

"The first dragon ghost I saw was sort of blue," Dudwin went on. "It had glowing eyes. And five spikes sticking up on top of its head."

"Is this a story, Dudwin?" asked LoLo.

"I don't know," said Dudwin. "But it's true."

"Now, Dudwin," said LoLo. "We all know ghost stories aren't really true."

"This one is," said Dudwin.

Dudwin's eyes reflected the orange flames of the campfire. It made Wiglaf shiver.

"After that, I started seeing ghosts all

over the camp," Dudwin went on. "And last night—"

"Stop!" cried Mordie. He jumped up from his camp stool and raced over to Dudwin. He steered the lad back to his place in the circle.

"I'm not finished!" cried Dudwin.

"Oh, yes, you are," said Mordie. "We don't want to scare the little ones." He patted Dudwin's head.

"Fie on Mordie!" muttered Dudwin as he sat down next to Wiglaf.

"Since our ghost story tonight was so short," LoLo said, "let's end with a camp song."

"It wasn't short!" Dudwin called out. "I wasn't done!"

"Shush!" said Mordie, glaring at Dudwin.

Then LoLo and Belchie led the campers in singing:

"Oh, give me a camp,
Where the weather is damp!
And you cook your food stuck on a spike!
Where you always hear
Mordie yell, loud and clear:
'Come on, campers! Let's go on a hike!'
Camp Dra-go-non-ka!
Where the lads and the lasses do play!
Where you'll never see
Any grass or a tree,
And the skies are so cloudy all day."

Wiglaf sang along with the others.

But Dudwin only stared into the fire, brooding. He turned to Wiglaf. "I see ghosts right now," he whispered. "They are trying to tell me something. Do you believe me, Wiggie?"

"I do not know," Wiglaf said. "But I know that you believe you see them."

"Fie!" Dudwin muttered. "No one believes me. Not even you, Wiggie."

Dear Brother Dave,

I need your help. My little brother Dudwin thinks he sees ghosts at this camp. Is there anything in your library books about dragon ghosts on Dragononka Ridge?

Please write back soon!

Your student,

Wiglaf

Chapter 13

ooty-toot tooty-toot *TOOT.*

Wiglaf opened his eyes. It was the start of another dark and cloudy day at Camp Dragononka.

Angus groaned. "Why does the sun never shine around here? It's like night every day!"

"Up and at 'em, lads!" Plungie called.

Wiglaf got up. He looked around for Dudwin, but his brother had already left the tent.

Wiglaf and Angus were the last to make their way down the hill. Once more, they saw a crowd of campers standing by the flagpole. They were all laughing.

"What's so funny?" Angus asked.

Wiglaf saw something red flying from the top of the flagpole—but it wasn't the Camp Dragononka flag.

"'Tis Mordie's big red shorts!" cried Wiglaf. "Someone ran them up the flagpole!"

They joined the throng of laughing campers.

As he drew closer, Wiglaf saw black letters on the shorts that said: GO.

GO? Inside his head, Wiglaf heard Dudwin saying, "G-O. That spells 'go'?" Did his little brother have anything to do with this prank?

Now Mordie came out of his tent. His hair was rumpled. He was still in his dressing gown.

"What's so funny?" he said grumpily.

The campers burst out laughing.

Mordie looked around. At last his violet eyes lit upon his flying shorts.

"Good King Ken's britches!" he cried, his eyes bulging. "Those are my shorts up there!"

This brought on a new round of laughter.

Wiglaf spotted Dudwin darting through the crowd. He beckoned him over.

Dudwin ran over to Wiglaf. "Good joke, huh?" he said.

Wiglaf stared at his brother's hands. They were covered with black smudges.

"Dud, your hands," said Wiglaf.

Dudwin looked down. "Oops!" he said. And he took off running for the lake.

"Enough!" barked Mordie.

The campers stopped laughing.

Mordie looked around the circle of campers. "Who did this deed? Speak up!"

No one spoke up.

"Live in fear, deed-doer," Mordie said. "I shall find you. Torblad? Bring 'em down."

"Yes, sir!" said Torblad.

"Sir is for school," Mordie reminded him.

"Yes, Mordie!" said Torblad. He untied the

rope and began lowering the shorts.

"The shorts say GO, Mordie!" called Moose. "What does that mean?"

"It means GO to breakfast!" said Mordie. "Go on. Go!"

Later that morning, Mordie organized a race to the top of Dragononka Ridge. On his way back down, Wiglaf spotted his pig.

"Daisy!" he cried. "How glad I am to see you!"

"*E-may oo-tay,*" said Daisy. She began trotting along beside him as he walked toward Lake Leechalot for swimming practice. "*Iggie-way, an-cay ou-yay ummon-say Elnoc-zay?*"

"The speech spell for Tusker," said Wiglaf. "I had forgotten. Yes, Daisy. I shall summon him."

"*Oodie-gay!*" cried Daisy.

"And perhaps a wizard can help me figure out what is going on around here," Wiglaf added.

The two agreed to meet at the mud wallow just before campfire.

"*Anks-thay, Iglaf-way!*" said Daisy. She skipped off toward the wallow.

Wiglaf decided to skip swimming and look for his brother. But Dudwin was nowhere to be found.

At lunchtime, Wiglaf hurried over to Moose.

"Have you seen Dudwin?" he asked him.

"He walked up Ridgetop Trail with me this morning," said Moose.

"Gwen led a nature hike to the far side of the ridge," offered another camper. "I think Dudwin went with them."

Hearing this, Wiglaf felt a little bit better.

Right before campfire, Wiglaf set off to meet Daisy. But Angus stopped him by the flagpole.

"You have to help me!" he said.

"With what?" asked Wiglaf.

"I think I know who stole all of my marsh-mallows," Angus said. "Come with me."

"Not now, Angus," Wiglaf said. "I promised to meet Daisy and Tusker at the mud wallow."

"Please! I beg of you! It has to be now," said Angus. "It won't take long." He grabbed Wiglaf's tunic and began pulling him up the hill. "I need you to stand lookout," he added when they reached Mordie's tent.

"You think *Mordie* took your marshmallows?" asked Wiglaf.

"He's my only remaining suspect," said Angus, slipping a tiny torch from his pocket and lighting it. The lads ducked inside the tent. "I heard him asking LoLo how there could be a Marshmallow Roasting Night when he didn't have any marshmallows," Angus added. He pointed to the tent flap. "Peek out. If you see Mordie coming, say 'Uncle!' and we'll run out before he sees us."

Angus began going through Mordie's bags and packs and boxes.

"Hurry!" said Wiglaf. He did not want to think what Mordie would do if he caught them there!

After a few minutes, Angus said, "Nothing! Maybe he ate them himself."

"Let us go," said Wiglaf. "Daisy will wonder what has become of me."

"I just want to check his tunic pockets," Angus said.

Wiglaf heard parchment rustling.

"Egad!" cried Angus. "This looks like a treasure map!"

Wiglaf hurried over to Angus. He peered at a drawing on the parchment.

"That is Dragononka Ridge," said Wiglaf.

"Right," said Angus. "Complete with the giant stones on top. And look. Someone wrote a name on top of the map. C. Looey."

"C. Looey?" said Wiglaf. "Could it be Crazy Looey?"

"Yes!" cried Angus. "Crazy Looey was babbling about losing a map."

Angus flipped the parchment over. "Here is a verse!" He held the torch near the parchment, and the two lads read its message:

"On top of Dragononka Ridge,
Where slabs of stone reach to the sky,
Are buried bones of dragons who
Spread wings and flew in days gone by.

On top of Dragononka Ridge
Lie bones of dragons who once roared,
And underneath the dragons' bones
Are buried all their golden hoards.

On top of Dragononka Ridge
The ghosts of dragons guard their gold.
They guard it springtime, summer, fall,
And through the winter's icy cold.

On top of Dragononka Ridge
The dragon spirits guard their posts,
Except one night—midsummer's night,
When they fly off with other ghosts.

On top of Dragononka Ridge
When all the ghosts away have flown,
On that one night of all the year,
The dragons' gold is left alone.

On top of Dragononka Ridge
If you dig gold, then fear the worst!
For on your head shall surely fall
The dreaded Dragononka Curse!"

"Crazy Looey said something about a curse," Wiglaf whispered. "Remember?"

Angus nodded. "Mordie must have found this map," he said. "Or maybe he stole it."

"Now all the camp activities make sense!" said Wiglaf. "We are training to dig up the dragons' gold!"

Angus nodded. "So that's what Uncle Mordie means by the BIG DIG."

Just then, the lads heard voices outside the tent.

"Yikes!" cried Angus. "Campfire must be over!" He stuck the parchment back into Mordie's pocket and tamped out his torch. "We have to get out of here!"

Wiglaf heard a voice calling his name:

"*Iglaf-way! Iglaf-way! Ere-whay are-yay ou-yay?*"

Wiglaf gasped. He'd forgotten about Daisy!

My Darling Poopsie Pie,

A thief at your camp! How awful!
Here's a double-big goodie box for you, my dear.
Remember—sharing makes the marshmallows taste
twice as good!

Smooches to my Poopsie!

Mother

Chapter 14

Wiglaf raced out of Mordie's tent. "Daisy!" he called, chasing after her.

The pig turned toward him, frowning. *"Ere-whay ere-way ou-yay?"*

"'Tis a long story," Wiglaf said. "Where is Tusker?"

"At-yay e-thay allow-way," said Daisy.

"Let us go there now," said Wiglaf. "I shall summon the wizard."

As all the campers headed for their tents, Wiglaf and his pig crept down to the wallow. There was Tusker, dozing in the mud.

"Usker-tay!" Daisy said. *"Ook-lay o's-whay ere-hay."*

Tusker opened one eye and grunted.

In the time-honored way of summoning wizards, Wiglaf chanted his name backward three times: *"CONLEZ, CONLEZ, CONLEZ!"*

A bright light flashed. And a blue-robed wizard stood before them.

"Vaaaark!" Tusker cried, jumping up.

"You again, Woolwig!" cried Zelnoc.

"Close enough," said Wiglaf. "Wizard, will you put a speech spell on Daisy's friend, Tusker?"

Zelnoc glared at Tusker. Then his eyes brightened. "Say, Wigwort, any chance you can pay me for this job?"

"Sorry," said Wiglaf. "We have no money."

"Bats' breath!" Zelnoc muttered. "The thing is, I broke Zizmor's brand-new cloud-maker. Total accident. But Ziz says I still have to cough up the price of a new one. I'm desperate for cash. Anyway, Wizard Rule

#598 says I can't turn down a request. So, let's get started."

The wizard began to walk around Tusker.

"Yawwwk?" said Tusker, his beady eyes on the wizard.

Zelnoc drew a wand from the sleeve of his robe. He pointed it at Tusker and chanted:

"Oink-a-la, doink-a-la,
Two, three, four!
Make this boar
A talking boar!"

Zelnoc touched Tusker's bristly head with his wand.

Tusker shuddered and blinked his beady eyes. Then in a deep voice he said, "I smell sausages."

"You have an excellent snout, boar!" cried Zelnoc. "I was frying sausages for my supper when I was summoned!"

"Got any on you?" asked Tusker.

"Alas, no," said Zelnoc.

"*Elnoc-zay!*" cried Daisy. "*Usker-tay eaks-spay English-yay!*"

"He speaks English." The wizard nodded. "What of it?"

"*Y-whay ot-nay Ig-pay Atin-lay?*" asked Daisy.

"He's not a pig," said Zelnoc. "And there's no such thing as Boar Latin."

Wiglaf couldn't get over it. Zelnoc had finally cast a spell that worked perfectly!

"Anything else?" said the wizard. "Or can I get back to my sausages?"

"There is something else," said Wiglaf.

Wiglaf quickly told Zelnoc what he had learned from the verse on Crazy Looey's map.

"Mordie wants us to dig up the dragons' gold on midsummer's night, when the

dragons are gone," Wiglaf explained.

"Gold?" said Zelnoc, perking up. "Why, if I could get some of that gold, I could pay Ziz back."

"No!" cried Wiglaf. "There is a curse on anyone who digs up the dragons' gold."

"Midsummer's night, you say?" asked the wizard.

Wiglaf said, "Yes, but—"

"See you then!" cried Zelnoc. And in a flash, he vanished.

Tusker turned to Daisy. "So," he said. "Don't you think my gold-tipped tusks make me the most terribly handsome boar you ever saw?"

Wiglaf left Daisy and Tusker beside the mud wallow and set off for the lads' tent. He was anxious to see if Dudwin was back from the nature hike.

Wiglaf hurried through the camp. He had not realized it was so late. He seemed to be the only one still out and about.

Wiglaf entered the lads' tent quietly so as not to disturb the sleepers. He crept over to where Dudwin slept. He reached out and patted his brother's blanket. There was no one under it.

Wiglaf shook Angus. "Wake up!" he said.

Angus sat up. "What? Has the thief been back for my new goodie box?" He felt under his bedroll and breathed a sigh of relief.

"Dudwin is still missing," Wiglaf whispered. "You must help me find him."

"All right," Angus said, getting up. "But I'm taking this with me." He slid an enormous goodie box out from under his bedroll.

The two crept from the tent. Angus lit

his torch and they headed for the trail. They had not gone far when they saw a group of campers coming toward them.

"Wiggie!" cried Erica.

"We got lost on our nature hike!" said Janice.

"Not lost," said Gwen, sounding annoyed. "Just a little confused."

"Is Dudwin with you?" asked Wiglaf.

Gwen shook her head. "No, it was just the three of us."

"What are you and Angus doing out here in the middle of the night?" asked Erica.

"Dudwin is missing," Wiglaf said. "We are trying to find him."

"We didn't see him up on the Ridge," said Erica.

"Maybe he was hiding," Wiglaf said.

"I shall help you find him, Wiggie," said Erica.

"Me, too!" said Janice.

"I'm going to get some shuteye," said Gwen. "Good luck!"

Wiglaf, Angus, Erica, and Janice set off. By now, they were so used to climbing the trail that they had no trouble doing it with only small torches to light their way.

"Dudwin!" Wiglaf called as they went. "Duuuudwin!"

But the little lad never answered.

As they hiked up the trail, Angus told the lasses what the verse on the parchment said.

"Mordie sure is going to a lot of trouble to get gold," said Janice. "He should sell swamp land for a ton of money like my dad did."

By the time they reached the foul-smelling top of the ridge, everyone was coughing. It was too foggy to see much. They all called and called. But Dudwin never answered.

They left the trail and began looking in the woods. Wiglaf called Dudwin's name until he was hoarse. They searched for hours.

At last they came to a clearing, and Angus said, "I cannot go on without a snack."

"I have some jerky from the nature hike," said Janice.

"And I brought these!" said Angus. He pulled the lid off his goodie box. Dozens of bright white marshmallows shone in the torchlight.

"You mean you're sharing?" asked Erica.

"You each get three," said Angus.

Suddenly, Dudwin appeared in the clearing.

"Dud!" Wiglaf croaked. He raced over to his little brother and threw his arms around him. "I was so worried about you!" Then he frowned. "Why did you not answer?"

"The ghosts froze me like a statue," Dudwin said. "I couldn't talk."

"Stop making things up, Dud," Wiglaf said.

"Wait," said Angus. "Remember when I couldn't swing the axe? Maybe the ghosts froze me. Maybe he's telling the truth."

"I am!" said Dudwin, nodding. "Hey, can I have some marshmallows?"

"Take three," said Angus. "Everybody gets three."

"Let's make a fire and toast them," said Erica.

Janice and Wiglaf gathered wood, and Erica made a fire. Angus found five toasting sticks. He stuck three marshmallows on each.

"Dudwin, did you run Mordie's shorts up the flagpole?" Angus asked as he handed him his stick.

"Tell the truth," said Wiglaf.

"Yup." Dudwin grinned.

"That's the best thing that's happened at camp all summer." Angus stuck three more marshmallows on Dudwin's stick.

They all held their sticks over the crackling fire. The scent of toasting marshmallows filled the air.

"Dud, why did you take off without telling me?" asked Wiglaf.

"I was mad because you don't believe me," said Dudwin. "But I *can* see ghosts. And I can hear them talking."

"I believe you now, Dud," said Wiglaf. "Really, truly I do." And he told Dudwin about the verse.

"It said anyone who digs up the dragons' gold will be cursed," Wiglaf finished.

"We must stop Mordie," said Angus.

Janice snapped her gum. "But how?"

How indeed? They were all quiet then, thinking.

At last Wiglaf said, "Dudwin, why is it that you can see and hear what we cannot?"

"Born lucky?" said Dudwin.

"Could be," said Wiglaf.

"Maybe I have special powers," said Dudwin.

"What about that dragon fang necklace you always wear, Dud?" said Janice. "Maybe it's magic."

"Shhhh!" said Dudwin. Then he whispered, "I see a dragon ghost right now."

One of Wiglaf's marshmallows floated up off his toasting stick. It hovered in midair. A blue flame whooshed from out of nowhere. It quickly toasted the marshmallow, and then the marshmallow vanished.

"Yikes!" cried Angus, Erica, and Janice.

"Zounds!" cried Wiglaf.

Suddenly Angus's goodie box began to rise from the ground.

"Noooooo!" cried Angus. He leaped up, lunging for his precious marshmallows.

But the box floated out of his reach. Up it went, stopping just above the tree tops.

"Give it back!" Angus wailed. "I beg of you! Give me my goodie box!"

A thought popped into Wiglaf's head. "Quick, Dud," he whispered. "Let me have the fang necklace."

Dudwin pulled off his necklace and put it over Wiglaf's head.

Wiglaf looked up. Hovering above their heads, he saw what looked like a large cloud. A large, dragon-shaped cloud. Not a cloud—a ghost. A dragon ghost!

My dear Wiglaf,

I haveth copied out these pages from _The Encyclopedia of Dragons_ for thee, lad. Thou art in grave danger. Diggeth not up that gold!

Thou faithful,

Brother Dave

The Dragononka Dragons

History: For thousands of years, the Dragononka Dragons ruled a large territory north of the Dark Forest.

Behavior: These strong, big-boned hill-dwellers were expert flamers. They often set fire to hillsides just to watch them burn. They never stole from humans, but delighted in stealing gold from cave-dwelling dragons and swamp-dwelling dragons.

Wealth: Over the years, the Dragononka Dragons amassed huge hoards of gold. They flew their loot to the top of a hill that they particularly enjoyed flaming. It became known as Dragononka Ridge.

Burial Customs: When Dragononka Dragons died, they turned to dragon dust, except for their bones, fangs, and claws. The surviving Dragononka

Dragons flew the remains of their dearly departed to the top of Dragononka Ridge. They buried the bones of their dead with their golden hoards, scattering their claws and fangs on top.

Extinction: After centuries, the Dragononka Dragons died out, but the ghosts of this mighty band still haunt Dragononka Ridge today.

Ghostly Temperament: The Dragononka Dragon ghosts are playful and peaceful—except when treasure hunters come to dig up their gold. Then, to protect their gold, the ghosts flame like mad and chant the dreaded Dragononka Curse.

The Dragononka Curse:
Don't ask!

Ghostly Appearance:
Body: see-through blue
Scales: silver
Horns: a fan of head spikes
Eyes: orange
Snout: powerful sense of smell
Fangs: prone to decay from eating sweets

Most Often Heard Saying:
"Keep your claws off my gold!"

<u>Biggest Surprise</u>: On
midsummer's night, the
Dragononka Dragon ghosts
leave the ridge and fly off to
the All-Spirits Ball, returning
only at dawn.

<u>Secret Weakness</u>:
Cannot resist the scent of
marshmallows.

Dear Mother,

I need more marshmallows right away. Send me as many marshmallows as you can. Do it today! This is an emergency. I'll explain when I see you.

Your son,

Angus

Hey, Mom and Dad!

Can you please send me all the marshmallows in Gildengeld? It is very important. I'll tell you why when I get home. If I get home.

Give Bibs a kiss for me.

Love,

Janice

Dear Mother and Father,

Please order the royal servants to buy up every marshmallow in the kingdom, and have the Royal Coachmen drive them to me as soon as possible.

I shall tell you why anon.

Do not delay!

Love,

Erica

Dear Brother Dave,

Thank you for your fast reply. The facts from <u>The Encyclopedia of Dragons</u> were a big help! We have a plan now.

Do you and the other Little Brothers of the Peanut Brittle ever make marshmallows? If so, would you make some and send them to us right away? It is a lot to ask, I know. But we are desperate. Midsummer's night is less than a week away.

Wish us luck!

Your grateful student,

Wiglaf

Hallo, Wiggie!

Sorry to take so long to answer you. It was not so easy to talk the postal peasant into taking down this letter in exchange for a bushel of cabbages.

So you are off at camp, enjoying yourself, eh? Taking it easy? Do they have such camps for older folks, such as myself? Get back to me on this.

I know you'll want a new joke to tell all your friends, so here goes:

Knock-knock!
Who's there?
Goblin.
Goblin who?
Goblin food gives you a bellyache.

'Tis a good one, eh? All right, one more.

Knock-knock!
Who's there?
Queen.
Queen who?
Queen up this mess!

Har har!

Your mother says to thank you for making her a bracelet. But she says blue stones bring bad luck, and wonders could you make her a bracelet from the shiny yellow metal known as gold?

Your brothers are fighting and biting, and your mother's run out of salt again. That's all the news from home, lad.

BURP!

Fergus

Captain, Pinwick Belching Team

Chapter 15

I hear thunder," said Wiglaf a few days later, as he and the other campers sat around the Campfire Circle cooking their breakfasts.

"Looks like rain," said Angus. "But then, it always looks like rain around here."

"You think Mordie will have the Big Dig if it rains?" asked Janice.

"He doesn't care if we get cursed," said Angus. "Why would he care if we get wet?"

"Have we got everything?" asked Erica.

Wiglaf nodded. "Are you ready, Dud?"

Dud sat with his arms crossed on his chest. "I guess," he said.

"It all depends on you," said Erica.

Dudwin touched his necklace. "I know," he said sadly.

"We shall try our best to get it back for you, Dud," Wiglaf said.

Just then Mordie strode in to the campfire circle.

"Great news!" he boomed. "Tonight is the Big Dig!"

"Yay!" cheered Gwen and Zelda and most of the campers.

But Wiglaf and his friends did not cheer.

"Here's how it works," Mordie went on. "I've buried some camp gold on top of the ridge."

"Real gold, Mordie?" called Moose.

"No," said Mordie. "Definitely not real. Camp gold is fake gold. So no point in you campers holding on to any of it. Got that?"

The campers nodded.

"Mordie is lying through his gold-filled

teeth," whispered Angus.

"You'll go up to the top of the ridge and dig as fast as you can all night long," Mordie went on. "You shall fill up sacks with gold, and run them down the hill to me. Then you'll go back up for more. The team who brings me the most gold will win one hundred dragon points!"

A cheer went up again: "Yay!"

That night after dinner, Wiglaf and the other campers walked down the hill to Campfire Circle. A great pile of logs had been laid. But no fire was burning. Dudwin sat down beside Wiglaf.

Mordie called out: "Stand for the Dragononka Fire Lighting!"

All the campers stood up. No one knew what was going to happen.

Then Axe Man, wearing his hood as always, ran into the circle holding a torch. He put the torch to the pile of logs and they burst into flames. Axe Man tossed his torch into the fire. Then he bowed toward Mordie.

Mordie turned slowly in a circle, eyeing all the campers. His violet eyes sparkled.

"This is the night you have been waiting for," he said, his voice low. "The night of the Big Dig. May the best team win."

"That's the Swamp Dragons!" yelled Zelda.

All the Swamp Dragons cheered and coughed.

"Cave Dragons rule!" yelled Gwen.

All the Cave Dragons coughed and cheered.

"Swamp Dragons, get a buddy and line up to my right," said Mordie. "Cave Dragons, buddy up and line up to my left."

Dudwin ran over and picked Moose for a buddy.

Wiglaf and Angus lined up together. Janice and Erica lined up behind them. Each of them wore a bulging backpack.

YoRick gave each pair a torch.

"Swamp Dragons, light your torches," Mordie said.

The Swamp Dragons held their torches over the blazing fire and lit them. Then the Cave Dragons did the same.

"Now follow me!" cried Mordie.

"Wait!" cried Dudwin. He ran to Mordie.

"Wait?" boomed Mordie. His violet eyes flashed angrily in the firelight. "For what?"

"For a good-luck charm," Dudwin said.

"Good luck?" Mordie smiled. "I like the sound of that! Especially tonight. Give it to me, lad. Be quick about it!"

Wiglaf's stomach was a knot. Could they count on Dudwin to do his part in their plan?

Dudwin took off his dragon fang necklace. Angus and Janice darted out of line and gave the little lad a boost, and he placed the necklace around Mordie's neck.

"Thank you!" boomed Mordie. "Come on, campers! Let's go on a hike!"

Mordie and the campers started up Ridgetop Trail.

Gwen and Zelda led the campers in singing as they hiked in a torchlight parade.

"Hail! Hail! Camp Dragononka!
We pledge ourselves to thee!"

The torches gave little light, but Wiglaf and his friends could have hiked up this trail blindfolded by now. This was their seventh trip up that day.

As they neared the top, the familiar stink grew stronger. Everyone started coughing even harder.

At last, Mordie bellowed, "Stop!"

In the flickering torchlight, Wiglaf could see the huge stones sticking up above the fog.

"Here ye go, lad," said YoRick. He handed Wiglaf a shovel. "Your buddy can hold the torch while you dig. Then switch."

Wiglaf, Angus, Erica, and Janice quietly slipped their packs off their backs.

"Oh, I really don't want to do this," moaned Angus. "It is not natural!"

"It's for a good cause," Wiglaf reminded him.

Angus nodded unhappily as he opened his pack and began tossing marshmallows into the air.

Wiglaf, Erica, and Janice spread out and

did the same.

"What are you doing?" asked Zelda when she saw them throwing marshmallows every which way.

"It's a Cave Dragon thing," Janice told her. "For luck."

"Listen up, campers," called Mordie. "Everybody start digging under a giant stone. That's where you're likely to find the gold. The fake camp gold, I mean."

"It smells really bad up here tonight, Mordie," said Moose.

"I just stepped in something sticky," said Torblad.

Mordie ignored their complaints. "Places, campers!" he shouted.

The campers raced to different stones.

"On your mark..." said Mordie.

The campers put their shovel blades to the ground.

"Get set..." called Mordie.

The campers put a foot on their shovels.

At that moment, Wiglaf called out, "CONLEZ! CONLEZ! CONLEZ!"

A flash lit the sky.

"Zounds!" cried the campers as a blue-robed wizard floated down and landed next to Mordie.

"Egad!" cried Mordie. "What are you doing here, wizard?"

"I was summoned," said Zelnoc. "And in the nick of time, from the looks of it."

"A wizard!" called out Moose. "Awesome."

"Thank you." Zelnoc took a little bow.

"Be gone, wizard!" cried Mordie. "We are in the middle of the Big Dig!"

"Then I'll bet you'd like to borrow this," said Zelnoc. From his wide wizard's sleeve, he pulled a shiny silver shovel. He pushed a small button on the handle, and the shovel blade began to spin like a drill. "I call it the E-Z Dig," he said, handing it to Mordie.

While Zelnoc babbled on, as they knew he would, Wiglaf and his friends kept tossing marshmallows until their packs were empty.

"I can't believe I didn't get to eat a single one!" Angus said as he tossed his last marshmallow into the air.

"Now we must wait," said Wiglaf. He thought he heard a distant flapping noise. But perhaps it was only the wind.

Mordie switched the E-Z Dig on to high. "This'll come in handy. Now leave us, Wizard. Scat!"

"Scat?" cried Zelnoc. "Scat is for cats. Not for wizards. No, if you want to get rid of a wizard you have to chant a Wiz-B-Gone spell. Oh, and it helps to be a wizard."

Mordie ignored him.

The flapping noise grew louder.

"I think it's them," whispered Wiglaf.

"Campers!" cried Mordie. "On your mark! Get set! Aaaaaaaaaaaahhhhhhhhhhhhh!"

Mordie covered his head with his hands and screamed again.

"Mordie!" cried Moose. "What's wrong?"

Mordie just kept screaming.

"What's happening?" cried the campers. "What's going on?"

"Bats and belfries!" cried Zelnoc, looking skyward. "Looks like an army of them!"

Mordie was running in circles, yelling, "This is the one night! You aren't supposed to come back until dawn! Go away! Shoo! Leave us alone!"

"Who's he shouting at?" cried Gwen.

"We are doomed!" Torblad yelled, and he burst out crying.

"Whoa, I've never seen such angry-looking ghosts," exclaimed Zelnoc. "There's got to be an easier way to pay Ziz back. I'm outta here!"

And in a flash, he was.

The campers huddled together in small bunches. In the confusion, most of them had dropped their torches and they had gone out.

"Please! Please! Don't hurt me!" cried Mordie. He squeezed his eyes shut and fell to his knees.

Wiglaf saw his chance. He raced over to Mordie and whisked the fang necklace off over his head. Mordie was so terrified, he never noticed.

Wiglaf put on the necklace and looked up.

"Zounds!" he cried. His eyes grew wide.

Erica and Janice raced over to him.

Dudwin and Angus were right on their heels.

"The sky is filled with dragon ghosts!" cried Wiglaf. "Hundreds of them!"

"I told you so!" Dudwin cried in triumph.

"It worked!" cried Angus. "All the marshmallows lured them back here."

"Their eyes are glowing," Wiglaf went on. "I can tell they're really angry."

"Let me see, Wiggie," said Dudwin.

Wiglaf quickly passed the necklace to him.

"Yowie!" cried Dudwin. "They're mad, all right. And they're chanting something, Wiggie. Something about...a curse. A curse upon our heads!"

"Sacks!" called Erica.

Wiglaf, Dudwin, Janice, Erica, and Angus dashed off in different directions. They ran to where they had hidden big sacks filled with marshmallows. Now they held the sacks above their heads and started running. As they ran, thousands of marshmallows spilled into the air above Dragononka Ridge.

Wiglaf shook the last marshmallow from his sack and looked up. He smiled. For everywhere he looked, he saw marshmallows that seemed to be floating up into the air all on their own.

"They've stopped chanting!" called Dudwin.

Small bursts of blue flame lit up the sky. And the smell of toasted marshmallows filled the air. The blue flames gave a surprising amount of light.

Mordie still knelt on the ground. He stared up into the blue-flamed sky. He looked like a frozen statue. A statue with big tears running down his cheeks.

"Run back to camp!" Wiglaf called to the huddled campers.

"Swamp Dragons, follow me!" called Zelda.

"Cave Dragons, let's go!" called Gwen.

The campers ran after their captains down Ridgetop Trail.

"We'd better go, too," called Janice.

"Wait!" cried Angus. "We can't leave Uncle Mordie up here."

"Ew, he stinks!" said Dudwin.

Wiglaf saw why—Mordie was covered in ghost slime.

"Uncle, come with us," Angus said in a soothing voice.

He and Wiglaf helped Mordie to his feet.

"The ghosts will soon be done with the marshmallows," Wiglaf said. "We must hurry, sir!"

"Sir is for school," Mordie babbled as the campers led him down the trail. "Here at camp, you can call me Mordie."

Chapter 16

I cannot believe camp is over," said Wiglaf as he spread his thin brown blanket out on the ground and started packing.

"The last day of camp," said Angus. "The summer sure went fast."

"I loved camp!" cried Dudwin, rolling up his royal blue blanket. "I want to come back next summer."

Wiglaf put his lucky rag, his sword, and his water flask on his blanket and bundled it up. He slipped the blue stone bracelet he had made for his mother into his pocket. Maybe if she saw the bracelet, she would change her mind about blue stones.

A gong sounded.

"Hooray!" cried Angus. "Our very last breakfast-on-a-stick!"

The lads and lasses ran out of their tents and down the hill to Campfire Circle. But instead of passing out the usual-on-a-stick, Cookie had made a huge pot of...something.

"What is this stuff, Yo?" asked Dudwin, peering into the pot. "It looks like dirt!"

"That's just the topping," said Cookie. He brushed the topping aside to reveal what looked like extra gooey mud.

"Ewwww!" cried Gwen. "It's got a worm in it!"

"It's got lots of worms!" cried Torblad.

"Try it," said Cookie. "You'll like it."

Angus bravely stuck a finger into the goo and licked it. "Mmmm," he said. "Tasty!"

Now LoLo came into the circle, leading Mordie. He did not look well. A dip in Lake

Leechalot had gotten the ghost slime off him. But now strands of green lake scum hung from his hair and beard.

"Mordie!" called Moose. "Which Dragon team won?"

"Dragon team?" said Mordie as if he'd never heard of Dragon teams. LoLo lowered him onto his camp stool.

"I was just about to make that announcement," said LoLo.

The campers held their breaths. This was the big moment.

"Since the...uh, event last night had to be canceled on account of strange weather," LoLo said, "the teams have the points they had going into the event. Cave Dragons..."

Gwen crossed her fingers.

"...have a total of 625 points," said LoLo.

"And Swamp Dragons?"

Zelda close her eyes and mouthed, *Please,*

please, please.

"...have a total of 625 points," said LoLo. "It's a tie! You're all winners!"

The campers erupted in cheers. They jumped up and down and hugged one another.

"We won!" cried Torblad, bursting into tears of joy.

"LoLo!" called Moose. "Do we all get a valuable prize?"

"That's a bit of a problem," said LoLo. "We didn't count on a tie. So we don't have enough patches for all of you. But we've found something even better than patches."

"What? What?" cried the campers.

"Something that will always remind you of your summer here at Camp Dragononka," said LoLo. "YoRick? Please pass out the prizes."

YoRick began making his way around

the Campfire Circle with a large, bulging bag. He stopped in front of Dudwin.

"Take one," he said.

Dudwin reached eagerly into the bag. He pulled out a shiny black rock.

"A rock?" he cried. "I have a hundred of these!" He tossed his rock back into the bag.

A few campers took the rocks. But most shook their heads when YoRick came by.

Mordie wobbled to a stand. "Farewell, campers," he said. "If any of you want to come back next summer, let me know. We could try the Big Dig again."

"I'll come, sir!" said Torblad.

Mordie smiled fondly at him. "Good lad," he said.

"Well, all right!" said LoLo, as if everything was. "Now, let's sing the camp song one last time."

"Hail! Hail! Camp Dragononka!
We pledge ourselves to thee!
There's no camp like Dragononka,
With its stumps of trees!
In Lake Leechalot you'll paddle,
Hike on Ridgetop Trail!
Outdoor fun for lads and lasses.
Dragononka, hail!"

As the song ended, everyone jumped up, ready to go home.

"I have to go tell Moose good-bye," said Dudwin, and he ran off.

Now Daisy trotted over to Wiglaf.

"Was it hard to say farewell to Tusker, Daisy?" Wiglaf asked her.

Daisy shrugged. *"Usker-tay is-yay ery-vay andsome-hay,"* she said. *"Ut-bay e-hay is-yay a-yay ore-bay."*

"So Tusker the boar is a bore." Wiglaf

smiled. Now a fancy golden coach rumbled through the Camp Dragononka gate.

"My ride's here!" Erica shouted, jumping up. "Come on, Janice! You, too, Angus! My coachmen can drop you off on the way back to the Royal Palace." She turned to Wiglaf. "You and Dud and Daisy come, too. The coachmen won't mind going on to Pinwick."

"*An-cay I-yay ay-stay at-yay e-thay alace-pay until-yay ool-schay arts-stay?*" Daisy asked Erica.

"Sure, Daisy," said Erica. "My mom and dad will be glad to have you at the palace." She turned to Wiglaf. "The coach will be a little crowded, but who cares? As we go, we shall make plans for what we'll do when we get back to good old DSA."

Erica raced off to greet the coachmen.

Wiglaf sighed. He had not told anyone that he would not be going back to DSA in the fall. He took the blue stone bracelet from his pocket. His mother would never wear a bad-luck bracelet. Perhaps he should give it to Erica. That way, she would have a token to remember him by.

Dudwin walked sadly over to Wiglaf. "I'm going to miss all the Swamp Dragons," he said.

Just then Zelda ran by. She saw Wiglaf holding the bracelet. "I was so busy being captain of the Swamp Dragons, I didn't have time to make anything for my mom," she said. "Any chance you want to sell that bracelet?"

"Sell it?" said Wiglaf.

"Seven pennies," said Zelda.

"Um—could you make it eight?" asked Wiglaf.

"Sure," said Zelda. She reached into her pocket and pulled out a fistful of pennies.

"Sold!" said Wiglaf as Zelda dropped eight

pennies into his palm.

Wiglaf grinned. "Eight pennies! Just what I need to go back to DSA!"

"I want to go to DSA, too!" said Dudwin. "Hey, Zelda? You want to buy a dragon fang necklace?"

"My dad will love that!" said Zelda. "Eight pennies?"

"Sold!" said Dudwin. He turned to Wiglaf. "Now I can be with you at school, too, Wiggy. Isn't that great?"

Wiglaf didn't answer. Instead, he started running toward the Royal Coach. Dudwin and Daisy ran right behind him.

"Hey, Erica!" Wiglaf called. "Wait for us!"

THE END

CAMP DRAGONONKA

HERE ARE SOME FUN THINGS FOR YOU TO DO IF YOU GO TO CAMP THIS SUMMER!

Goldius est goodius!

WIGLAF'S GHOST STORY

This ghost story is great to tell around a campfire!

THE RING OF TRUTH

Badlance loved gold more than anything. One day he and some other campers went on a nature hike on the far side of Dragononka Ridge. Badlance left the others and went off on his own to hunt for gold. Near the mouth of a cave, he spied a ring with a large red stone. When he picked it up, he saw something written inside the ring. It said "The Ruby Ring of Truth."

"Oh, Ruby Ring of Truth," said Badlance. "Do you always tell the truth?"

The ring answered back: "No lie have I ever spoken."

Badlance shoved the ring onto his finger.

"Oh, Ruby Ring of Truth," said Badlance. "Where can I find gold?"

"Inside a chest in Long Lost Palace," said the ring.

"Oh, Ruby Ring of Truth," Badlance said. "How do I get to Long Lost Palace?"

"Walk to Vulture Valley," said the ring.

Badlance set off for Vulture Valley. When he lost his way, he asked the ring for directions. The ring always told him the right way to go.

It grew dark. Badlance kept walking. At last he came to the top of the hill. In the moonlight, he saw a palace below—Long Lost Palace.

Badlance hurried down the hill. He could see vultures perched on the palace's turrets. Bats flew in and out of its windows. Badlance shivered. He did not like the looks of Long Lost Palace. Still, he wanted gold. He pushed open the door.

Creeeeeeeak!

It was very dark inside. It smelled like old, wet boots.

Badlance lit a torch and nearly screamed! The place was covered with huge spiderwebs. A big, fat spider sat in the middle of each web.

Badlance loved gold even more than he feared spiders. So he walked farther into the palace. At last he came to a door.

He opened it.

Creeeeeeeak!

When he shone his torch, dozens of mice ran into their holes.

Badlance loved gold even more than he feared mice. So he hurried through the room to another door. He opened it.

Creeeeeeeak!

Hundreds of rats stared at him with glowing red eyes.

Badlance was deathly afraid of rats. But he loved gold more than he feared rats. So he ran through the room to another door, while rats tried to bite his ankles.

Badlance opened the door.

Creeeeeeeak!

He found himself in a long, narrow hallway. There were no spiders. Or mice. Or rats. At the end of the hallway was a long, low chest glowing with golden treasure.

"Golden Treasure!" he cried, and he ran toward the chest.

But as he drew near, Badlance saw what was glowing.

Not a treasure chest...

It was a coffin!

Badlance stared at the glowing coffin. And as he did, the coffin rose from the floor and hovered in midair.

Badlance was frozen with fear!

Then the coffin turned, all on its

own, and started floating straight at him.

"Ahhhhhh!" Badlance screamed.

He turned and ran!

The coffin floated after him.

Badlance ran through the room with rats.

The coffin floated right behind him.

He ran through the room with mice.

The coffin floated right behind him.

He reached the room with giant spiderwebs.

The coffin floated right behind him.

He ran for the door. He could feel the red hot glow of the coffin on his back.

Suddenly, Badlance remembered the ring.

"Oh, Ruby Ring of Truth!" he cried. "How can I stop this terrible coffin?"

And the ring replied, "Take a cough drop!"

ERICA'S CAMP CHEERS

There were lots of cheers for Camp Dragononka. You can make some up for the camp you go to.

These are my cheers:

Cave Dragons! Cave Dragons!
Rah! Rah! Rah!
Swamp Dragons? Swamp Dragons?
Ha! Ha! Ha!

Cave Dragons breathe fire!
Cave Dragons breathe smoke!
Swampies think they can beat us.
We say, what a joke!

One Swampie! Two Swampies!
Three Swampies, four!
You think you can beat us?
Better think some more!

Swamp Dragons! Swamp Dragons!
Wading through the ooze!
Swamp Dragons always win!
Cave Dragons lose!

Hey nonnie nonnie and a ho ho ho!
Camp Dragononka is the place to go!
Do we like it? Y-E-S!
Camp Dragononka—it's the best!

We added a second verse:

Hey nonnie nonnie and yuck yuck yuck!
Camp Dragononka is the place we're stuck!
Do we like it? Say it loud and clear:
Camp Dragononka—get us out of here!

Janice's Camp Songs

> We sang some really crazy songs at Camp Dragononka! Here are two of my favorites!

100 Flagons
(Sung to the tune of "100 Bottles of Beer on the Wall")

100 flagons of mead on the wall,
100 flagons of mead!
If one of those flagons should
happen to fall...

99 flagons of mead on the wall!

99 flagons of mead on the wall,
99 flagons of mead!
If one of those flagons should
happen to fall...
98 flagons of mead on the wall!

(Keep singing until there are no flagons left—
or until you're too hoarse to sing anymore!)

At Camp Dragononka
(Sung to the tune of "On Top of Old Smoky")

At Camp Dragononka,
When supper draws near,
The campers start shaking
With dread and with fear.

While Cookie was chopping
Some meat that was hot,

He whacked off his thumb and
It fell in the pot.
Cookie cried, "Egad!
My thumb's in the stew!
If you find it, campers,
Remember—don't chew!"

He put on a bandage,
But that fell in, too,
So at Camp Dragononka—
BEWARE OF THE STEW!

Angus's Dirt Cake Recipe

Have you ever eaten DIRT CAKE? It sounds bad, but it tastes good. Trust me!

You'll need:
- 1 package Oreos
- 1 8-oz. tub of Cool Whip
- 2 boxes instant chocolate pudding
- Milk for pudding
- Gummy worms
- Pan or clean flower pot
- Vanilla cookies

1. Put the Oreo cookies in the freezer overnight. (Makes them easier to crush.)

2. When you're ready to make your DIRT CAKE, have an adult help you crush the Oreos in a blender or in a plastic bag with a rolling pin or mallet.

3. Follow the directions on the box to make the instant pudding. Make sure an adult helps you.

4. Put the Cool Whip into a bowl. Add pudding to it until the mix is a nice dirty color. The more pudding, the darker the DIRT CAKE.

5. Put a layer of the Oreo "dirt" at the bottom of the pan or flower pot.

6. Pour the pudding mix over it. Add more Oreo "dirt" in the middle to make layers. You can put gummy worms in the middle, too.

7. Sprinkle the rest of the Oreo "dirt" on top to cover the pudding mix.

8. Make dragon tombstones out of vanilla wafers. Slip the wafers into the cake so that only their top halves stick out.

9. Decorate the top of the DIRT CAKE with gummy worms coming out of the dragon "graves" in front of the tombstones!

10. Ask some friends over to help you eat DIRT CAKE! (But not too many friends or there won't be much left for YOU!)

OUR FAVORITE CAMP
KNOCK-KNOCKS

Knock, knock!
Who's there?
Canoe.
Canoe who?
Canoe get me out
of here??

Wiglaf

Knock, knock!
Who's there?
Hero.
Hero who?
Hero the boat across
Leechalot Lake.

Erica

Angus

Knock, knock!
Who's there?
Howard.
Howard who?
Howard you like to take a hike?

Zelda

Knock, knock!
Who's there?
Dragon.
Dragon who?
Dragon this canoe isn't easy.

DRAGON SLAYERS' ACADEMY™ 18

NEVER TRUST A TROLL!

Wiglaf is thrilled to be returning to DSA as a
Class II lad! But he's less thrilled that his wild little
brother Dudwin is joining the school, too. And
he is not one bit thrilled when his Class I "Little
Buddy" turns out to be an overgrown troll who tells
great big whoppers and thinks it's funny to play
tricks on people—particularly on Wiglaf.